SQUAD

Stand Up
and Cheer

SQUAD

Stand Up
and Cheer

by Lara Bergen

SCHOLASTIC INC.

ISBN 978-0-545-56280-5

Text copyright © 2013 by Lara Bergen
Megaphone art throughout © inkytycoon/iStockphoto

All rights reserved. Published by Scholastic Inc.
SCHOLASTIC and associated logos are trademarks
and/or registered trademarks of Scholastic Inc.

12 11 10 9 8 7 6 5 4 3 2 1   13 14 15 16 17 18/0

Printed in the U.S.A.   40
First Scholastic printing, September 2013

THREE CHEERS FOR TEAM DELANEY —
JACKIE, JORDAN, AND DENISE!

CHAPTER 1

"Mom! Where are they? I think we left them!" Kendall hollered from her new room.

Panicked, she bounded down the stairs, skipping the last three, and bolted to the right. Then she stopped. Wait. This wasn't the way to the kitchen, she realized. Would she *ever* get used to this new house? Quickly, she spun and ran the other way, dodging boxes as she did. At last, she burst into the kitchen. Her mom looked up and grinned.

"Hey, you! I was just thinking how nice it would be to have your help," she said.

Kendall's mother was standing beside the kitchen counter, surrounded by moving boxes, some open and some still taped closed. She was wearing shorts and a tank top, and yet she still had a damp spot in the middle of her back. The air conditioner, it seemed, was broken, and it was *hot* in their new house. All along the counter next to her were stacks of dishes she'd just unpacked. She peeled a sheet of newspaper off a drinking glass and set it next to them. She tossed the crumpled paper into an empty box all the way across the room.

"Yes!" she said. "Two points!" She glanced at Kendall and frowned playfully. "Boy, you're hard to impress. . . ."

"Mom!" Kendall groaned. "I can't find any of my trophies. I think they got left in New York."

"Oh, honey, I'm sure they're somewhere," her mom assured her. "Look at all these boxes we still have to go through." She gestured to the dozens just in the kitchen, which were only a fraction of what filled the house — a house that Kendall hadn't seen, aside from in pictures her dad had showed her, until they'd pulled into the driveway that afternoon.

Thirty-six hours before, Kendall had been a New Yorker, living in an apartment near Central Park. Now, she guessed, she was a "Midwesterner," living in a house with a backyard. Before, she'd shared a room with her little sister. Now she had a bedroom all to herself. It had a window seat and shelves built into the wall . . . which would have been great if she'd had her gymnastics trophies to fill them with.

But no. Now she had nothing to remember New York by. Nothing to remember her friends. Nothing to remember the biggest part of her life for the past eight years.

Well, okay. Maybe she had a ton of pictures. And maybe she had been texting with her friends pretty much constantly for the past two days.

She wasn't forgetting anything — and her friends weren't forgetting about her.

But still.

"I know we left them! I know it! We have to go back — now! *Please*," she begged.

Her mom blinked a few times, then closed her eyes and slowly shook her head. "They're somewhere," she said calmly. "And we'll find them. Just relax. Have you looked through the other boxes?"

Kendall shook her head. "No. But I wrote 'Trophies' and 'Kendall's Room' on the box, and put a bunch of green stickers on it."

All the boxes with green stickers were supposed to go in her room, along with her desk, her green swivel chair, and her half of the bunk bed. "That was the whole point of color-coding all the boxes, wasn't it? To tell the movers where everything went."

"You'd think," her mom said. "But things happen." She sighed. "Why don't you look around? I'd like to be sure they're not here before we drive a thousand miles back to New York. Or better yet" — she held her arms out — "why don't you unpack a few of these boxes with me? Who knows? Maybe they'll turn up. Besides, hon, remember, they're just trophies. I thought you were done with gymnastics for now."

There was really nothing for Kendall to say to that, so she simply shook her head. Parents. They always talked about how they understood — but really, they never did. It was true that even before her dad got a new job in a new city and announced they were going to move, she'd already decided to take a break from gymnastics after the state finals back in May. It took up so much time. And then there was her wrist sprain, which she still felt sometimes, and her recently pulled hamstring. There was also the growth spurt she'd had in fifth grade — two inches in three months — which had changed everything. Uneven bars, which had been fun for so long, were suddenly tough. Mounting the balance beam was easier . . . but so was falling off. That was a big part of why her old trophies mattered so much to her now. Who knew? They might be the last ones she earned for a very, very long time.

The night before, in the motel sofa bed, she'd lain awake, staring at the ceiling and wondering about just that. Would she find something she was just as good at in Fairview, the town that would be her new home? Was she going to fit in there, or would she stick out like a five-foot-tall sore thumb?

"Where's Dad?" Kendall asked, sighing.

"He went out to get some food. Hey, have you asked Libby about your trophies?" her mom suggested. "She's always good at finding stuff."

"No," Kendall replied slowly. But that was a good idea. "Libby!" she yelled, dashing back to the staircase. "Have you seen my trophies, Lib?"

Unlike their old two-bedroom apartment, their new house had four. There was basically a room in each corner of the second floor, off a hall shaped like a square U. Kendall's parents got the big one with its own bathroom. Because she was older than her nine-year-old sister, Libby, Kendall got the next-biggest room, in the shady back corner of the house. Libby got to choose from the two that were left. She picked the sunny one, diagonal from Kendall's, closest to the bathroom they would share. She was in her room now, crouched on the floor in front of two plastic pet carriers.

When people first met Kendall and her sister, they always said they looked alike. They had the same coffee-colored skin and the same big brown eyes. Kendall's nose was slightly wider than Libby's, but they both had the same round tip. Kendall liked to wear her hair back, or up, and Libby usually did the same. That day Libby had it loose, however, so her curls hid her face as she leaned over the open crates.

"Come on, guys," she was saying softly. "You can come out. You don't have to be scared."

Inside, Kendall knew, were Tiger and Lily, their two shell-shocked tabby cats. This hadn't only been the cats' first move, it had been their first car ride, and it had been hard. Lily, who was gray and white and much more vocal, had cried throughout the two-day trip. Tiger, candy-corn-colored and usually silent, had been perpetually carsick.

Now they were equally quiet, and eerily still.

Kendall knelt down beside her sister and reached into Lily's crate. "Have they come out at all?" she asked as she rubbed the back of Lily's silky neck.

Libby shook her head. "Not even to eat or use the litter box. I hope they're okay," she said.

"They're fine," Kendall assured her. "They just have to get over the shock. Maybe you should give them a little space." She scratched behind Lily's ear, then pulled her hand out and leaned back on her heels.

"Okay." Libby scooted back, too, but her eyes never left the cats. She waited a second for some sign of movement, but when it didn't come, she leaned in again. "Please come out," she begged. "You don't know what you're missing, guys. You have a great big house with stairs and everything to run around in now."

"Seriously, Lib," Kendall said. "Give them some time. They'll come out when they're ready. You're making it worse doing that, I bet."

Libby looked back at Kendall over her shoulder, one eyebrow raised, just like their dad. This was a skill, like tongue rolling, that Libby alone had inherited.

"I'm not making it worse. Did you need something?" Libby asked.

"Actually, yes." Kendall was used to her sister's attitude, so she tried to ignore her and get to the point. "I packed a box full of all my trophies. Have you seen it, by any chance?"

"Oh, sure." Libby nodded.

"You have?" Kendall gasped. "Where?" She scanned the boxes stacked in Libby's room. There weren't that many, maybe six. They all had purple stickers. STUFFED ANIMALS was neatly written on the side of one. The others were graffitied with LIBBY'S BOOKS! VERY FRAGILL! KEEP OUT!

"I told the movers to put it in the basement," Libby said.

The basement? "Why?" Kendall asked.

"Because. When you have a house with a basement," Libby explained, "that's where trophies go."

Kendall didn't even know where to start with that one. "Uh, no. Actually, they don't."

"Oh, yes, they do," said Libby. "In every book I've read."

"Well, clearly you haven't read any books about *me*, Lib," Kendall said.

Libby shrugged and went back to hovering over Tiger's and Lily's crates. "Sorry," she said. "I was just trying to help."

Kendall sighed as she got to her feet. She was too relieved to be mad. She moved to the door, then paused and turned. "Have you tried treats?" she asked.

"Do we have some?" asked Libby.

Kendall shrugged. "I'll check, and if we do, I'll bring them up."

"Hey, girls! Kendall! Libby!" Suddenly, their mom's voice vaulted up the stairs. It sounded different in this box-filled house than it had in their old, cozy home.

"Yeah!" Kendall called back.

"Come down here, will you, girls?"

"Do I have to?" Libby yelled, sitting up. "I'm giving therapy to the cats!"

"Yes," their mom answered. "You do! Don't make me wait!"

Libby sighed and stood up.

"Come on, they'll be fine," Kendall said, draping her arm around Libby's thin back.

Halfway down the stairs, Kendall saw her mom standing just inside the open front door. She was holding a large white envelope and standing next to a wispy-haired blond girl. The girl was shorter than Libby, but still looked about her age. She had pink shorts over a bright yellow bathing suit, and a rosy, freckled face.

"Libby, Kendall, this is Claudia. Guess what?" said their mom. "She lives next door. I just went out to check the mail, and I met her and her mom."

"Hi." The girl smiled, making instant dimples.

"Hi." Libby smiled back.

"My mom's going to turn on the sprinkler. Want to come over?" Claudia asked.

"Uh . . . okay." Libby shrugged.

"Do you have a bathing suit?" Claudia asked.

"To watch the sprinkler?"

"No, to run through it!" Claudia laughed. "That's the whole point. To get wet."

"Oh!" Libby understood suddenly. "Like the fountain in the park! Can I do it, Mom?"

"Of course," their mom said. "Ooh . . ." Then she bit her lip and paused. "The only thing is I'm not quite sure where the bathing suits are packed."

"She can borrow mine," Claudia offered.

"I can borrow hers!" said Libby. "Did you hear that, Mom? All right?"

"All right! Go, then!" their mom said, giving Libby a quick hug. "Have fun, girls. Libby, tell Claudia's mom, Mrs. Berman, thank you, and be good! Okay?"

"Hey, what about your cat therapy?" Kendall couldn't help teasing her sister as Libby followed Claudia outside.

"They'll be fine," said Libby, waving with confidence. "They just need a little time."

The girls skipped off, and Kendall's mom turned to her. "You look happy. Find your trophies?" she asked.

"I hope. Libby thinks they're in the basement." Kendall and her mom exchanged a *figures* smile. Then Kendall nodded to the envelope still in her mother's hand. "What'd we get in the mail our first day here?" she asked.

"It's from your new school. Here, open it. I don't know what it could be. Let's hope something good!"

Her new school. *Ugh.* The words flipped a switch in Kendall that made her stomach do the twist. School didn't start for several weeks, but — who knew? — maybe in Fairview they went ahead and sent their class lists out early. How nice it would be to know the names of the kids she'd be going to school with, Kendall thought. Maybe some even lived nearby and were hoping to make new friends — like her. Or better yet, maybe the school had a big end-of-summer, before-school-started, welcome-the-new-kids good-old Midwestern picnic!

Just please don't make it summer reading or homework, she wished.

Kendall pulled a stapled packet out of the envelope and read it together with her mom.

Fairview Middle School Cheerleading Tryouts

Go Fairview Falcons!

Kendall read it again. "They have *cheerleaders* in *middle school*?" she said, surprised.

"Hmm . . ." said her mom. "Things are different here than in New York, I guess, huh? Oh, look, it says they cheer for football and basketball games . . . and other school events. That's kind of cute." She shrugged, peering at Kendall. "Interested?" she asked.

Kendall flipped through the pages of the packet. Cheerleading? She'd sure never considered doing *that* before. She imagined herself in one of those outfits and giggled at the thought. But then again, maybe the idea wasn't so crazy. From the little bit of cheering she'd seen, she thought it did look like a lot of fun. Plus her gymnastics experience, she knew, would be a very good thing. It even said right there in the "each candidate will be scored on" list that tumbling could earn you ten whole points.

"I don't know," she told her mom slowly. "Do you think I'd be any good?"

"I think you'd be good at anything you put your mind to," her mom said automatically.

Kendall rolled her eyes. She wondered if parents had to memorize lines like that at the hospital before they brought their babies home.

"I'm serious, Mom. They score a lot for tumbling, and I can definitely do that. And it says they have clinics to help you with the other stuff all week, Monday through Thursday, then tryouts on Friday afternoon. Oh, wow," she realized as she read, "it starts next *week*!"

That was soon!

But also good.

She'd kind of been dreading the upcoming weeks before school started, with no one to hang out with and nothing to do. She could text and video chat with her friends back in New York, of course, but it wasn't the same. At all. At the very least, she thought, she could meet some girls her age at the clinics and hopefully make friends. And at the most, she could end up a cheerleader after tryouts — and *really* blow the minds of all her friends back in New York!

"I think I should do it. Can I?" she asked.

"Sure." Her mom shrugged. "I'll call today and sign you up. It'll be a big commitment, you know, when you're just getting used to a new school. But I think you'd be really great, and I bet you could meet a lot of girls."

It took Kendall a second to process the "yes" at the heart of all that, but she hugged her mom as soon as she did. "That's just what I was thinking, Mom! Exactly!" she said.

Beep! Beep! Just then, a silver car pulled into the driveway. It was her dad back from some restaurant with two huge bags full of food.

"Dad!" Kendall took off down the brick walkway before he even opened his door. "Dad, guess what I'm going to try out for!"

CHAPTER 2

Fairview Middle School was big. Kendall couldn't even see it all at once. She was used to city schools, the kind that were huge but went up instead of out. This one stretched along the street like an airport, but with all the doors in one place — under a giant carport, on which was written the school's name.

The sides were deep brick red, and the roof was bright ocean blue. All around it was thick green grass that smelled sharp and freshly mowed.

The school had been quiet and even lonely-looking when Kendall's family drove by the week before.

"There it is," her dad had said, pointing. "Kendall's new school!"

This afternoon, though, was different. The semicircle driveway was filled with a long line of cars. Girls of all shapes and sizes hopped out of them, but they were all dressed alike: white shirts, black shorts, white shoes and socks, and high, tight, spring-loaded ponytails.

Kendall checked hers in the car mirror before she opened the passenger door. (Riding shotgun was definitely the best perk, so far, of now being nearly as tall as her mom.)

She managed a smile. "Do I look like a cheerleader?" she asked her dad.

"That depends," he said, then grinned. "What does a cheerleader look like again?"

"I guess we'll find out," said Kendall, trying to sound like she didn't care. Clearly, though, her flickering smile gave her butterflies away.

"You know, hon" — her dad rubbed her shoulder — "you don't *have* to do this, if you don't want. I know you're hoping to make some friends, but you'll meet plenty of kids when school starts."

"I *want* to do it," she told him quickly. "I just don't want to make a fool of myself."

He nodded. "Tell me about it. I know exactly how you feel."

"You do?"

"Kendall, honey, I felt the same way — exactly — this morning, at work."

It had been his first day at his new job as the morning DJ at WXFV. Kendall had listened to his whole show in the kitchen with Libby and her mom.

"Really? But you didn't sound nervous at all," she said.

"Why, thank you," he said with a wink. "That's the beauty of radio, I guess. That and" — he pointed to his T-shirt and shorts — "I can go to work in this. But it never gets easy, I'll tell you, starting new things."

"So what did you do?" asked Kendall.

"The same thing I always do," he said. "I took a deep breath and counted to ten and asked myself why I was there. And when I answered, 'Because I want to be,' I told myself, 'Well, okay, then, make the best of it. Get out there and do your best.'"

Kendall took a deep breath.

She counted to ten.

Then she looked at her dad.

"Go get 'em, tiger!" he said. "Or whatever they call themselves here."

"The Falcons, Dad." She smiled and reached for the door handle.

"Right. Go Falcons!" He blew her a kiss. "See you at six."

There were signs leading Kendall and all the other girls around to the side of the school. There, above two huge blue doors, was the simple word "GYM." Taped to one door was a poster saying CHEER-LEADING TRYOUTS IN HERE!

Inside, it was chilly from air-conditioning, dance music was playing, and girls were already jumping around. Two older girls sat at a table and asked Kendall for her name with wide, eager smiles.

"Hi, Kendall! I'm Jackie," said the one with thick, glossy black hair, as she made a checkmark on a list.

"And I'm Jordan. First tryouts?" asked the other, who was blond and slightly sunburned. Some might even say "sun-kissed."

Kendall nodded.

"Awesome!" said Jackie.

"Good luck! You'll love it!" Jordan declared. Then she glanced at the clock just above the scoreboard, high on the far gym wall. "Go ahead and stretch if you want," she told Kendall. "We'll be starting right at four."

Stretching was a good idea, Kendall thought. But the dozens of mats were all full. She finally spotted some space on one in the corner and made her way over as fast as she could.

"Um, hi," she said to the girl sitting there. "Can I share your mat?"

The girl looked up at her with big brown eyes, smooth, round cheeks, and two delicate moles: one was just above her left eyebrow, the other just to the side of her nose. Her hair was dark, and thick, and straight, and very, very long. Even in a high ponytail, it fell almost to her shorts.

"Sure," the girl said, revealing bright silver braces. "Of course." She scooted over to make room.

"Thanks," said Kendall. She sank down with her heels together and her knees out to the sides. "I'm Kendall," she went on after a second, hoping to break the ice. "I just moved here."

"Cool." The girl smiled slowly. "I'm Sophia. I'm not new, but I am new to this school. I'll be in sixth grade," she said, sounding hopeful.

"Really?" said Kendall. "Me too!" She unfolded her legs into a split and smiled as she stretched from side to side.

"Wow, you're really limber," said Sophia, wide-eyed. "You've done this before, I guess."

"Oh, no, never," Kendall said quickly. "I don't know anything about cheerleading — yet. Do you?"

Sophia bit her lip and looked sorry. "Not really. Just what I've seen online."

"YouTube?" Kendall asked.

Sophia nodded.

"That's so funny." Kendall giggled. "Me too."

FWWWEEEEEEEEEEE!

Both girls jumped and twisted around at the sound of a whistle across the gym. The woman who had blown it stood under the score-board, her hands in fists and on her hips. She was wearing blue track pants and a white T-shirt with a "Fighting Falcon" on the front. Her blond hair skimmed her shoulders and was held back firmly by bobby pins.

"Hello, athletes!" she said. "I'm Coach Casey!" She waved. "Which, if you were on the squad last year, you know all too well. Of course, if you weren't, you still might recognize me from the library — where, by the way, I am still Ms. Kent. But here in the gym," she continued, "I'm a hundred percent coach — a hundred percent *cheer*. Which is what I hope you all are, too. So tell me, everybody: Who's ready to work hard this week and have a lot of fun?"

About half the gym clapped and hollered as Kendall and Sophia looked around. Coach Casey, meanwhile, crossed her arms, shook her head, and frowned.

"I'm sorry. . . . Let's try that again. I said: Who's ready to have some FUN?"

Kendall traded smiles with Sophia, and together they shouted, "WE ARE!" with the rest of the gym at the top of their lungs.

Coach Casey smiled and nodded and returned her hands to her hips. "Now that's more like it!" she said, satisfied. "Now we can really get on with the show. We're here to show our spirit, after all, right?" She cupped her hand to her ear.

"Right!" echoed the crowd.

"Very nice! You know what I'm talking about! Okay, Jackie and Jordan, come on up here." The coach signaled the girls who had checked Kendall in, and waited for them to jog up. "Jackie and Jordan were our squad captains last year, for those of you who might not know."

"Yay, Jackie! Yay, Jordan!" a group near the front cheered as the two girls waved back with both hands.

"Now, of course, they're in ninth grade and getting ready to cheer for Fairview High. We're going to miss them a lot, that's for sure," Coach Casey said. "But let's thank them for coming back this week to help lead the clinics for us, okay?"

This time, Kendall and Sophia both yelled "YAY!" without a prompt.

"They'll also be judging with me at tryouts on Friday," the coach went on. Then she paused. "Tryouts." Her eyes scanned the room. "Some of you have done it before, of course. If you have, welcome back. You all know the drill. For those of you who are new this year, though, let me explain how it all will work. First of all, every day, just like today, we'll start at four o'clock sharp. Don't be late. No excuses."

Kendall sighed. Coach Casey already reminded her of her old gymnastics coach, who had the same passion for her sport. She liked to say things like "It's gymnastics, not gym*nice*tics," and "If you're not sore, you're not working hard enough."

"After roll call, we'll warm up," the coach continued, "then we'll spend some time on motions and jumps. At this point, as far as I'm concerned, you're all starting out in exactly the same spot. There are sixty of you and you *all* have a shot at being one of the twenty we pick for the team. If you can tumble, definitely bring that."

Yes! Kendall thought.

"But don't worry if you can't. Spirit. Attitude. That's what the sport's really about, and that's what we, the judges, will be looking out for most of all." She clapped. "As far as today goes, we'll be focusing on the dance routine. Tomorrow, we'll teach you the cheer, then we'll work on both for the rest of the week."

Kendall turned to Sophia, who was pulling her ponytail under her chin. Their eyes met and they traded smiles that said, *This is going to be intense!*

"Okay!" The coach clapped. "Let's get started with some warmups. Everyone up for jumping jacks!"

After the jumping jacks, there were toe touches, then stretching. The coach led them in a lot of the same things Kendall had done in gymnastics. And then, as promised, Coach Casey had Jackie and Jordan demonstrate the most basic cheer skills.

"First, some motions," said Coach Casey. "Notice how they're starting with their hands straight and tight by their sides? This is called clean. Ready, Jackie and Jordan? Okay! Let's begin!"

She began by calling out hand positions: "*Buckets!* Fists. Thumbs to the ground. *Candlesticks!* Fists. Thumbs to the front. *Blades!* Fingers straight. Again, thumbs out in front."

Then she moved on to arms: "*Touchdown!* Arms straight up. Thumbs facing in. *Clasp!* Hands together. Thumbs in front of your chin. *High V!* Arms straight up and out. *T!* Arms straight out to the sides. Make sure your thumbs are to the ground. Lock those elbows. No. Noodle. Arms!"

Jackie and Jordan demonstrated each and every motion, smiling as they did. They reminded Kendall of synchronized swimmers — only without the pinchy-nose things and sparkly swim caps.

"Notice how strong and tight they are?" said Coach Casey. "You want to *snap* into every move!"

Wow, Kendall thought. That was so different from the graceful, fluid moves her coaches had always stressed in her gymnastics routines.

"We'll be looking for tight, sharp motions at tryouts," the coach warned, "along with perfect posture . . . and a big smile, too, of course!"

That, at least, Kendall was used to: smiling till her cheeks cramped up and got numb.

"Good job!" Coach Casey told her assistants. Then she pointed both hands at the girls who'd been watching quietly. "Okay, everyone! It's your turn. And remember: Hit your motions slightly forward — like this — so you can see your arms."

Body positions came next — lunges and squats and kneels — and Kendall was happy to find that all her years of gymnastics helped a lot with these skills. She could see Sophia, beside her, stumble a little, but so did several other girls. She and Sophia were clearly not the only ones who'd never cheered before.

"Great work, everyone!" shouted Coach Casey. "Okay! Let's move on to jumps!"

To begin, Coach Casey had Jackie and Jordan demonstrate simple jumps — tucks, spread eagles, and one where they bent one leg in the front and one in the back, which they called a double hook. Then, just for fun, they showed off some fancier jumps, like toe touches, pikes, and hurdlers, and one they called a "herkie," which was like the toe touch, but with the front leg kicked straight out and impossibly high.

Next the coach broke the jumps down into steps: approach, lift, execute, and land. And finally, she split the girls into groups by grade and sent them off to give them a try.

Coach Casey took the sixth graders and led them in a tuck — bringing their knees up to their chests. "Good! Nice, high chins!" she said. "Use those arms to get you up!"

She had them do a spread eagle next. "Think of it this way," she told them. "Let your body make an X."

When Kendall's turn came, she tried to jump as high as she possibly could, and she even took the liberty of following up with a toe touch, which in gymnastics they'd always called a straddle jump.

She felt great when she came down! But Coach Casey looked less than thrilled.

"What's your name?" the coach asked, and Kendall told her — in a voice that was high and choked. "Okay, Kendall, that wasn't *bad*. You definitely got some nice height. But what happened to your approach and lift?"

Kendall could feel her whole body, even her knees, getting hot and red. "I forgot." She winced. There were some things, like jumping, she guessed, that she was going to have to learn all over again.

"That's okay." Coach Casey smiled. "That's why we practice. But if you don't do every step — from count one to eight, you're going to be off from the rest of the squad."

Kendall nodded numbly, wishing she could disappear. She was relieved when a tan, blond girl stepped forward and flashed a startlingly perky grin.

"Is this good, Coach?" she asked, whipping her arms into the air. She crouched down, then popped up, and out flew her legs, bringing her toes to her fingertips. She returned to earth, still smiling. "I'm Madison McElroy, by the way," she said.

"McElroy." Coach Casey gave the girl a knowing nod. "Of course you are. I see you've been learning a few things from your sister. How's Megan doing? Is she captain at Fairview High this year?"

"She is," replied the girl as she straightened the bow in her ponytail.

"Well, be sure to tell her hi for me," said Coach Casey.

The girl nodded dutifully. "So . . . how was my jump?"

"Oh, very good. Nice form. Definitely bring that to tryouts," the coach said. Then she noticed the time and reached for her whistle.

FWWEEEEEE!!!!!!

"Water break!" she called. "Five minutes, girls! Then back on the floor to learn the dance!"

Kendall hung back, and so did Sophia, as the other girls ran ahead. Kendall nodded to the girl with "nice form" and the bow in her hair.

"Wow," Kendall said. "She sure is good. I can't believe she's in our grade."

Sophia simply nodded.

"Do you know her?" Kendall asked.

"Kind of." Sophia shrugged. "I mean, everyone knows her. At least, everyone who went to our school. She's really . . . popular. It makes sense that she'd be here. She's nice, I guess, if she likes you. But we're not really . . . friends . . . you know." She nodded to the darker-haired girl walking beside Madison. Their ponytails swung in perfect time. "That's Mia, her best friend. They do *everything* together. They call themselves 'M and M.'"

"Really?" said Kendall.

"Uh-huh."

Wow. Kendall could see how tight they were. They walked arm in arm to the fountain and all the way back across the gym. Some girls waved and they said hi back, but they kept their giggles to themselves. They were basically stuck to each other like Post-its, Kendall thought, and she was pretty positive they would make the squad. In fact, they already looked like they belonged.

When the break ended, Coach Casey turned on the music — a song everybody loved — and she had Jordan and Jackie do the whole dance once for everyone to watch.

After that, they did it again, step by step, without the music, instead counting out loud from one to eight.

"Okay, girls, now you try," said Coach Casey. "Slowly. Go! One . . . two . . . three . . . four . . . five . . . six . . . seven . . . eight! Again! High V . . . Low V . . . K . . . Check . . . Lunge . . . Clasp . . . Diagonal . . . Punch!"

Oops! thought Kendall as she lunged when she should have hopped up.

"Attitude!" Coach Casey said, clapping. "Chin up. Back straight! It's time to say good-bye to shy and hello to the spotlight!"

Attitude, thought Kendall, *right*. But the more she thought about her "attitude," the more she found her hand or foot — or both! — going somewhere it didn't belong.

Out went her arms when everyone else's went down. *Clap!* Her hands came together just as the rest of the gym punched up.

Kendall's cheeks started to burn while, somehow, the rest of her body froze.

"That's okay, keep going!" the coach shouted. "Recover! Never stop!"

Kendall tried and looked over at Sophia, who seemed to be struggling a little, too. Then she made the mistake of looking at Madison, who was hitting every move. Of course, that only made Kendall less sure of every step and every clap. She hadn't expected to be *great* on the first day, but she didn't think she'd be *this* bad. The hardest part, she realized, was keeping up with rows of other girls. In gymnastics, there was no group to match. Whatever she did, it was just her.

Finally, at six o'clock sharp, Coach Casey blew her whistle and announced they were done.

"There was a lot of spirit out there! Both the dance and the cheer are on the school's website, so I *strongly* recommend you watch them. And *practice*. A *lot*! With a friend, if you can. Not only will you inspire each other, it's more fun than by yourself. Okay!" She clapped her hands officially. "So what are you going to do?"

"Practice!"

"How much?"

"A lot!"

With a sigh, Kendall turned to Sophia. "Well, see you tomorrow," she said. Then she suddenly got an idea and wondered if Sophia might be thinking the same thing. "Want to practice together? Tomorrow?"

Sophia looked surprised — but pleased. "Yeah . . . That would be great!"

"Awesome! Oh . . ." Kendall frowned slightly.

"What?" said Sophia. "What's wrong?"

"My house . . ." Kendall said. "We just moved . . . and, well, it's still a wreck."

"That's okay. We can do it at my place," said Sophia right away. "My mom has to work, but she won't mind. Oh! And bring your bathing suit. We can swim, too, if we have time."

CHAPTER 3

Sophia lived in an apartment between Kendall's new house and the school. It was different from Kendall's old apartment in New York, which had been on the eighteenth floor. Sophia's was on the first floor of a two-story building that looked a lot like a large house. Plus there was no lobby and no elevator. The front door opened right to the outside. There were several more buildings just like it spread out around a clubhouse and a peaceful turquoise pool. Multiple sprinklers misted neat rows of pansies, and as she walked along the sidewalk, they gently watered Kendall, too.

Kendall rang the doorbell and Sophia answered it, still in her pajamas, which were pink and black and short. Her long, loose hair covered her shoulders and most of her tank top.

"Hi!" she said to Kendall. "I was just getting dressed. Come in."

"Mmm." Kendall walked through the door, sniffing. "What smells so good?" she asked.

"Cinnamon rolls," said Sophia. "Want one? They're still warm."

She led Kendall into the kitchen, which was just big enough for a small table and two chairs. On the table were a pitcher filled with bright red tulips just starting to open up and a bowl full of peaches, nectarines, and plums.

"Here," said Sophia, offering Kendall a plate of cinnamon rolls. They were the kind with the white, creamy icing that came in a cardboard tube.

"I love these," said Kendall.

"I know," said Sophia. "Me too."

They each had one — and then another, just as Sophia's mom appeared. She had a big coffee mug in her hand that looked like a child had painted it.

"Mom, this is Kendall."

"Hi, Kendall. It's so nice to meet you." Sophia's mom put her coffee on the counter and held out her hand. She looked a lot like Sophia, Kendall noticed, only without braces and with much shorter hair.

"It's nice to meet you, too," Kendall said, shaking her hand, "Mrs. . . ." She paused.

"Arcella." Sophia's mom smiled and pointed to the name tag — MONICA ARCELLA — on her rose-colored uniform. "Sophia told me you just moved here."

"Yes," Kendall said. "From New York."

"Oh, I love New York," said Mrs. Arcella. "This is a big change for you, I bet."

Kendall nodded. "It is. But I like it so far." She smiled.

"Well, I think it's wonderful you're trying out for cheerleading. That'll be a great way to make new friends. I have to say, I was surprised when Sophia said she wanted to do this, but now I'm thinking it's a great idea. Just so long as it doesn't get in the way of your schoolwork. Right?"

"Right, Mom," Sophia said.

"Well," said Kendall, "my dad always says that the busier you are, the more you get done."

Sophia flashed her a grin as her mom nodded and said, "That's so true, isn't it."

She put her arm around Sophia's back and squeezed it. "Well, have fun, girls," she said. "I wish I could stay and watch you practice." She peered over Sophia's shoulder at her wristwatch and clucked her tongue. "Ugh, but I have to go. There's plenty of sandwich stuff for lunch. I probably won't be home before you girls leave, so make sure the door's locked, Sophia, if you go to the pool."

Sophia nodded responsibly. "Yes, Mom."

Her mom kissed her on the cheek and gave Kendall a quick hug, too. "Bye, girls. I'll see you later. Have fun — and be good!"

"Your mom's nice. Where does she work?" Kendall asked as the door clicked behind Mrs. Arcella's back.

"She's actually our school nurse," said Sophia. She offered Kendall the last sweet roll on the plate.

Kendall took it gratefully and began to unroll it into a long, cinnamony snake. "Really?" she said. "That's so cool. Is that where she's going now?"

"Oh, no." Sophia explained, "She gets the summer off, too. She's working at a nursing home right now. She fills in for the regular nurses who go on vacation and stuff like that."

"*That's* a switch from middle school," said Kendall, imagining all the walkers and gray hair.

"I know, right?" Sophia grinned. "But actually my mom says old people and sixth graders have a lot more in common than you'd think." She licked a spot of icing off her finger and put the empty cinnamon roll plate in the sink. "Let me go get dressed, okay? Then we can start practicing."

"One, two, three, four, five, six, seven, eight . . ."

"Okay," Kendall said, "I think we've got it. Let's try it with music. What do you think?"

Sophia made a face that said, *I think you're crazy*, but went ahead and clicked "play" on her computer.

The song came on and the girls tried their best to keep up with the beat. Within seconds, though, they were both impossibly off and fell, laughing, to their knees.

"I don't think we're ready for the music yet," Sophia said.

Kendall giggled. "Yeah, you're probably right."

"Hey, want to work on something else?" asked Sophia. "Like maybe the jumps — since we're going to have to do them in tryouts, and I can barely get an inch off the ground."

"Excellent idea," said Kendall, springing to her feet. She raised her arms. "How do those steps go again?" she began. Then she looked around and stopped.

There wasn't a ton of space in Sophia's bedroom. They'd had to keep their dance moves pretty small between her laptop and her bed. Kendall could just see herself trying to do a straddle jump — make that a *toe touch* — and knocking over Sophia's whole desk. Or her shelves, which were full of books. Or the trophies along her window-sill. Sophia had blushed when she'd told Kendall what they were for: "Math Olympics, and chess, and that one with the globe was for the geography bee last year."

"I'm thinking maybe we should go outside to do this," Kendall suggested, and Sophia readily agreed.

They went out through the sliding glass door in Sophia's living room to her sunny, fenced-in yard. Just outside was a cement patio with a charcoal grill and a picnic table surrounded by four white plastic chairs. Past that was thick green grass polka-dotted with dandelions.

"Just watch out for the garden," Sophia said, pointing to a squarish patch of tall tomato plants off to the side.

Even though it was hot outside, the grass felt cool on Kendall's bare toes. She couldn't help putting her hands down in it, too, and doing a happy front walkover.

"Wow!" exclaimed Sophia. "How'd you do that?"

"That?" said Kendall. "Oh, it's not hard."

"What else can you do?" Sophia asked.

"Um . . . ?" Kendall twisted her mouth and thought for a second. "I can do this." She reached back and did the reverse, a back walkover. "And this." She jumped up and backward, pulling her knees in, landing a solid, if rusty, back tuck.

"Omigosh! That's amazing!" said Sophia. "Where'd you learn to do *those*?"

"Well, I did a lot of gymnastics back home," explained Kendall. "I mean, back in New York."

"You have to do those at tryouts!"

Kendall nodded. "I thought I would. I'll need something to make up for my timing and my dancing." She grinned. "What kind of tumbling can you do?"

"Me? I can't do anything." Sophia pulled her hair close and bit her lip. "Do you think that'll be a big problem?" she asked. Kendall could tell she was worried.

"No, definitely not," Kendall assured her. "It's not a requirement, remember. Just do a cartwheel. That'll be totally fine."

"I can't do a cartwheel," said Sophia.

"Oh, come on." Kendall put a hand on her waist and cocked her hip out. "You're kidding. Let me see you try."

"Seriously. I'll show you," Sophia said.

She ran her fingers from her forehead back through her thick hair. Then she took a deep breath, bent down, leaned to her left, and did . . . *something*.

She was right, Kendall realized. That move had definitely not been a cartwheel.

"Okay." Kendall clapped like Coach Casey. She was not going to let Sophia stop there. "First of all, you're starting wrong. Here, let me show you what to do. First, stand up straight and point a leg out. Whichever one feels best. For me, it's my left. Now you put your arms up like this and lock your elbows — keep them super straight. Now, bend down and turn your shoulders so they're sideways, like this. The first hand you put down should be the same as the foot that's pointing out. Then *push* with that leg and kick with your back leg so you come to a handstand and split your legs . . . then twist and put your legs down one at a time . . . right, left — ta-da!"

Kendall finished her demonstration and stood with her hands in the air again. "You should look just like you did when you started, except facing the opposite way."

Sophia nodded slowly, frowning.

"Well, go ahead. Try it," Kendall said.

Sophia looked doubtful, but she did it. . . . At least, she tried to repeat Kendall's steps. Once again, though, something kept her feet from getting up and over her head.

"Can you do a handstand?" Kendall asked her.

Sophia murmured a wary "I guess."

"Okay, so maybe we should start with that," Kendall said, leading her around the tomatoes and to the fence. "Put your hands down," she said, "and kick your feet up here."

"I don't know." Sophia sighed. "I think it might be a lost cause."

"Don't be silly," Kendall told her, nodding toward the ground. "Go ahead. Hands down, feet up. You are going to do a cartwheel — even if it takes you all week to learn!"

CHAPTER 4

Kendall and Sophia practiced in the backyard, and they even practiced in the apartment complex's pool. Sophia still couldn't do a real cartwheel by the time they had to head to school, but their jumps and their dance routine had visibly improved.

At the cheerleading clinic, the dance was the first thing they reviewed. Jackie and Jordan stood in the front with their backs to all the girls. Slowly, they went through each eight count while the rest of the gym followed along. At the same time, Coach Casey wove in and out of the crowd, making corrections and giving advice: "Clap! Clap! Snap! *Snap!* That's it! *That's* it! Punch and kick! *Very* nice!"

She paused in front of Kendall and Sophia, who were standing side by side. Kendall stopped breathing as she waited for the coach to tell her she'd done something — or several things — wrong.

"Nice kick," Coach Casey said matter-of-factly. "That was really nice and sharp and tight. You too." She pointed to Sophia. "Nice posture. Very good. But don't look so serious. This isn't brain surgery. Remember, we're here to *cheer* up the crowd."

Sophia tried to smile, and so did Kendall . . . but then, of course, they totally lost count and forgot where they were.

Kendall wondered if they'd get to try doing the dance to music, but after a half hour of run-throughs without the song, Coach Casey announced they were moving on.

"Who wants to learn a cheer?" she called out.

"We do!" the girls all replied.

"Jordan? Jackie?"

The ninth graders stepped up and faced the clinic, smiling as if this were the moment they'd been waiting for all their lives.

"Watch carefully," said Coach Casey.

"Hit it!" they shouted. *Clap!*

"Who are you cheering for?

Fairview! Falcons!

Stand up and cheer once more!

Fairview! Falcons!

Louder now! Don't be shy!

We want to hear your Falcon pride!

FAIRVIEW! FALCONS!"

They finished with their fists planted firmly on their hips.

"Now let's do it again," Coach Casey told Jackie and Jordan, "but this time let's break it down." She pointed with both hands to the girls watching. "You guys clap with me and repeat the cheer as they go. Ready? Hit it!"

"Who are you cheering for?"

"Good! But cheer from here! The *diaphragm*!" Coach Casey called, grabbing her stomach with both hands. "You want to be loud, but you don't want to scream. And for heaven's sake, *smile*, girls! When I look at you, I want to think you've never had so much fun, even in your wildest dreams!"

When they'd gone over all the words, they added the motions, step by step. Then the coach announced they'd break into smaller groups and work on the cheer even more in those. She had them count off, one through ten, and Kendall and Sophia traded pouts. A three, Kendall waved *so long* to Sophia as Sophia scooted off to join her fellow fours.

There were six girls in Kendall's "three" group, and she recognized two: Madison and Mia — aka "M&M" — the girls she'd noticed the day before. How'd *they* get the same number, she wondered, when they'd been standing side by side?

She smiled as she walked up, but neither M smiled back. They were too busy fixing each other's bows and laughing at some private joke.

The other threes, who all looked older, greeted her with friendly waves.

"Hi, I'm Natasha," said the tallest.

"I'm Kiki," said another, who had more freckles than Kendall had thought a face could hold.

"I'm Ella," said the third. She smiled an easy smile, revealing an unexpected gap between her teeth. She also had a big plastic boot instead of a sneaker on her left foot. "Are you new?" she asked Kendall. "What grade are you in?"

"I am." Kendall nodded. "And I'll be in sixth."

"Cool. Welcome to Fairview. We'll all be in eighth."

"Thanks. Nice to meet you. I'm Kendall. You've all cheered before, I guess."

Ella nodded, and so did Natasha. "Yeah, we were on the squad last year."

"Too bad you have to try out again," said Kendall.

"Tell me about it." Ella grinned, running her tongue over her gap.

"I tried out last year, but I didn't make it," said Kiki. "*And* the year before."

"She's going to this year, though," said Ella, putting her arm around Kiki's shoulder. "If at first you don't succeed, try, try again. Right?"

"Let's hope. But don't jinx it," said Kiki warily.

"Don't worry," said Natasha. "I have a good feeling about it this year."

"Hey, guys?" Madison raised her hand and waved her fingers. She and Mia, it seemed, had deemed their bows good enough to go. "How 'bout we do this cheer?" She smiled and put her hands on her hips. "I mean, that's what we're here for, right?"

The older girls looked at each other. "Yeah, sure, let's do it." Ella shrugged. "How about I call it, okay?" She clapped. Then she followed the line from M&M's eyes down to her clunky boot. "Oh, don't worry about this," she said. "It doesn't even hurt."

"What *happened*?" asked Madison, looking mildly horrified.

Lily laughed and Ella blushed. "A horse stepped on my foot," she admitted. "I was wearing tennis shoes instead of boots. All my fault. I was totally dumb. But I go to the doctor tomorrow, and I should be able to get rid of it, I hope." She straightened into clean position. "Don't worry. I can still do everything in the cheer but jump at the end. Ready?" She looked around their little circle. "Okay, hit it!" she yelled.

Clap!

They went through the cheer once — *very* slowly, and Kendall felt pretty good. She knew her arms and legs didn't "pop" quite as much as everyone else's — except maybe Mia's — but she could work on that. She got all the moves down, and in the right order. That, at least, was good.

"A little faster this time?" Ella asked, and everyone nodded. "Okay."

So they did it again, a little faster, just as Jackie bounded up.

"You guys look awesome!" she said to the whole group, but to Ella
and Natasha she gave big, sisterly hugs.

"We're going to miss you so much!" moaned Ella. "Who'll be
our captains now? You were the best ever! Hey, what's high-school
cheer like?"

"Oh, *tons* more work!" said Jackie, loving it. "But we get to do a
lot more stunts."

"Base or flyer?" asked Natasha.

"Flyer!" Jackie grinned.

"My sister's a flyer, too." Madison spoke up. "*And* the captain of
the squad."

"Oh, right! You're Megan's sister!" Jackie pointed to her. "She is
so amazing! And she told me to look out for you and say hi."

"*Ah*, it figures cheering's in your family," said Ella. "Now I understand how you're so good."

Madison inhaled, looking pleasantly self-conscious, as if she
heard the same thing all the time.

"Hey, how's the coach?" Ella asked, turning back to Jackie. "Is
she as hard-core as they say?"

Jackie rocked her head in a *yes . . . and no . . .* kind of way. "She's really awesome, but yes, Coach Casey's basically a *librarian* compared to her."

"But she *is* a librarian . . ." said Kiki.

"It's a metaphor," Jackie explained.

"Wow," said Kendall. "And I thought this coach was pretty tough."

The older girls looked at one another and together shook their heads.

"Oh, Coach Casey might seem like a drill sergeant," said Ella, "but she's really great."

"Yeah, she's awesome. You'll love her," Natasha agreed.

"*And* she's looking at us!" Jackie warned, nodding behind them. "So how 'bout you run through the cheer again, you guys, and I'll tell you what I think?"

They took it from the top, and Kendall tried to remember this time to do everything she had to do . . . to keep her arms straight, and her wrists tight, and her smile big and wide. But when they got to the end and returned to clean, arms down, she was the first one Jackie picked out.

"So nice! But always remember, when you lunge," said Jackie, "pop your foot up, like this. And watch your fists. In a V, your thumbs are forward, but when you punch, they should go back. You too." She pointed to Mia. "And you don't want to rely so hard on watching Madison here. You'll get points off in tryouts if it looks like you don't really know the cheer. Now, do you sixth graders know about spiriting?"

Kendall wasn't surprised when Madison nodded and said, "Of course," or when Mia saw her and quickly bobbed her head, too. But that left her the only one, it seemed, who had no idea what "spiriting" was.

She had two simple choices then, she guessed: to ask what it was, or not. Both would be embarrassing . . . but one would help her learn at least.

"Uh . . ." She raised her hand slightly. "I don't know. What is it?" she asked.

"Of course," said Jackie. She turned to Mia. "You want to show her?" she asked.

"Me?" Mia suddenly looked as if Jackie had asked her to dribble her head. "Uh . . ."

"I'll show her. It's easy," said Madison. She cheerfully nudged Mia aside and clapped. Up went her arms and she wiggled her fingers, then pointed the first ones in the air. "Number one!" She pumped one fist, kicked — two times — and wound up, step by step, as the coach had shown them, into a pretty great toe-touch jump.

"Go, Falcons!" she shouted at last.

"Exactly!" Jackie applauded, and the rest of the group did, too. "Megan's taught you a lot, I guess, huh? Spiriting's just another — very important — way to pump up the crowd," she explained to Kendall. Her eyes cut to Mia, then returned. "We'll get to it later this week," she went on, "but we'll definitely be judging you on it, so it's a good thing to start practicing now. Jumps . . . tumbling . . . spirit fingers." She wiggled her fingers as she counted off. "There are tons of things you can and should do in tryouts. Don't be shy about throwing your best skills in, whatever they are. You know?"

"Like even a handspring or something?" asked Kendall.

"Sure," Jackie said. "Can you do one?"

Kendall answered by taking a deep breath. She checked behind her, then squatted low and sprang back into the air. Her hands hit the floor and she snapped her legs over, as she'd done hundreds of times in the past.

"Whoa! Definitely do that!" said Jackie. "You get big points for those kinds of things."

Jackie had to move on, but she told them to keep working and they dutifully did. And yet somehow it was different, at least for Kendall. It was like she'd suddenly grown an inch — which was just what she needed, evidently, to grab the attention of M&M.

Almost immediately, Madison pulled Mia up and introduced both of them to her. "If only I could tumble like you. Wow," she said.

Kendall wasn't sure how to respond at first. She felt as if Madison had turned a spotlight directly on her.

"Well, I wish I could jump like you," she said finally, which turned out to be just the right thing to say.

"Oh, thanks." Madison flicked her ponytail modestly. "It's not that hard, really," she went on. "It just takes practice, and I have been doing it since I was, like, three. But, wow, if I could do a back hand-spring . . . Wouldn't that be great?" She turned to Mia, who was already nodding but paused and started up again.

"Hey! What are you doing tomorrow?" Madison asked Kendall. "Before the clinic, I mean." She didn't wait for an answer but turned back to Mia. "She should come over, don't you think?"

Mia blinked and stopped nodding. The thought clearly took her by surprise. "Uh, sure." She looked at Kendall and smiled. "Yeah, totally. You should!"

"And tomorrow's a really good day," Madison went on, "because my sister, Megan, will be around. She usually has cheer camp, but she's home tomorrow, and she can coach us. She *loves* that so much."

Mia leaned in toward Kendall. "That's just another way of saying that she loves telling people what to do," she joked.

"Oh, don't listen to her." Madison elbow-nudged Mia, giggling. "Careful, Mia, or she won't want to come. So, twelve thirty?" she declared, as if it were settled. "I'll text you my address. Do you have a phone? We'll also work on hair," she added, taking Kendall's shoulders and gently twisting her around.

Kendall felt a light tug on the end of her ponytail.

"You're going to want to wear this higher," Madison said.

"*Much* cuter," Mia agreed.

"And you need a bow, of course," said Madison. "Do you have any? Don't worry if you don't. You can pick one out when you come over. I have a gazillion. Literally."

Kendall felt a "Great. Thanks!" gush immediately out of her mouth. A split second later, however, a thought seeped into her head. Sophia. She kind of had a plan already to practice with her the next day.

"Um, tomorrow . . ." Kendall said slowly. "Could Sophia come, too?"

"Sophia?" Kendall was still facing away from M&M, but she sensed their totally blank looks. "Sophia who?" they asked.

"Sophia Arcella? You know her, I think. She went to school with you last year."

The girls didn't say anything. Kendall slowly spun around. M&M were looking at each other with unenthusiastic frowns.

They didn't say no, but Kendall could tell the word was there, waiting to come out.

"Never mind," she said quickly, wishing she could take the question back. She knew very well — very, very well — that the choice she was making might not be *right*. But really. How could she pass up

47

an invitation to practice with a real high-school cheerleader? And hang out with the most popular girls in school at the same time?

"It was just an idea," she continued. "I'll ask my mom about tomorrow and I'm sure that she'll say yes."

"Great!" said Madison as a smile of relief appeared.

"So great," said Mia, nodding and smoothing back her hair.

Kendall smiled at them both, but at the same time, she felt a pain. It was the ache of knowing she'd have to tell Sophia she couldn't practice with her the next day.

CHAPTER 5

It wasn't so hard for Kendall to call Sophia on Wednesday and say that her plans had changed. "My mom has a million errands to do," she explained, which was 100 percent the truth. "And she needs me to go with her . . ." she added, which was not at all a fact.

But what else could she say? Kendall asked herself. She couldn't tell Sophia that she was going to Madison's but that Madison didn't want Sophia to come along. Besides, Sophia didn't really seem to care about being friends with Madison and Mia all that much. But Kendall was new and didn't really know anyone yet. How could she say no?

"Oh, that's too bad," Sophia said.

"I know," Kendall replied. "But you don't need me to practice your cartwheel. You can do that on your own, you know?"

"Yeah, I know. I will," said Sophia. "At least, I'll try my best."

"Great! Well . . . see you at practice," Kendall said quickly. "Gotta go."

But as soon as she hung up, she started to wish she hadn't lied. Her mom did have errands to run, but what if somehow, somewhere, Sophia saw her mom out doing them by herself? Or what if Sophia called Kendall's house and her mom was there and answered and told Sophia where Kendall really was?

Kendall was excited to make new friends, but she also liked the one she'd already made. She guessed that was why she couldn't shake the nagging, prickly feeling she was doing something she'd regret.

It was all she thought about on the way to Madison's and for the first minute she was there. But she quickly discovered the McElroy house was not a place you could worry in for long. First of all, there were way too many things to look at. There were columns and wall-paper, and layers of curtains and a very complicated chandelier, plus all sizes of shiny, polished tables covered with shiny, polished things, including dozens of silver-framed photos and a whole herd of china pigs. And that was just in the front hall, where Kendall entered by mistake.

"Oh, it's you!" Madison laughed when she opened the front door. She had a small silky dog in her arms with hair a shade darker than hers. It also had a bow to keep its bangs out of its eyes, and an eager, persistent bark. "I thought it was some salesman," said Madison. "No one ever comes in this way."

"Oh, sorry," said Kendall, flustered.

"No, no, that's fine. But next time you can just come in through the back door. *Shh*," she told the dog, setting it down on the ground. "That's enough out of you. Seriously."

The dog stopped barking, then started again, hopping up on its back legs.

"Oh, she's so cute!" Kendall knelt down to pet it. "You're a good girl, aren't you! What's her name?"

"It's a *he*, actually," said Madison. "And it's Herkie, I'm afraid."

"As in the jump?"

"Mmn-hmn."

"That's funny!" Kendall looked up, beginning to laugh.

Madison shrugged. "Yeah, it kind of is, I guess. But don't say that to my mom," she warned.

As if on cue, a figure appeared at the top of the stairs and began to jog gracefully down. Kendall had a feeling it must be Madison's mother . . . but she sure didn't look like an average mom. She was dressed almost like a cheerleader, except that her short, sleeveless dress was totally white. Around her head, she wore a spotless white visor, which perfectly matched her startlingly bright smile. She reminded Kendall of a movie star . . . or someone in a toothpaste commercial, at least. Her long blond hair was pulled back tightly and wrapped with a stiff white bow, even bigger than Madison's, that seemed to defy gravity.

Herkie instantly dropped to all fours and raced, panting, to her feet. She bent down, scooped him up, and let him lick her cheek.

"Hello!" the woman said, rising and greeting Kendall, who was already standing back up. "Who's this, Madison?"

"This is Kendall, Mom. She's new. And she's trying out for the squad."

"Oh, how *wonderful*!" said her mother. "Did you cheer at your old school?"

"No, never," said Kendall. She suddenly hoped that was okay to admit.

"Oh, poor you." Mrs. McElroy clucked and slid out her bottom lip. "But better late than never, as they say! We don't know what we'd do without cheering, do we, Madison?" She glanced at Madison briefly to be sure she nodded, then zeroed in on Kendall again. "But don't let anyone tell you it's just about being cute or popular. Those are just side effects. What can you do? It's about dedication and commitment to yourself, and to your squad — who are, by the way, *the best friends* you'll make in your life, you know."

Off to the side, out of her mom's view, Madison was rolling her eyes and mouthing along. Kendall knew better than to laugh, but clearly Mrs. McElroy gave this speech a lot.

"So have you met Megan yet?" she asked Kendall.

"No, I haven't," Kendall replied.

"Well, aren't you in for a treat!" Mrs. McElroy declared as she set Herkie back down on the rose-covered rug. His feet sank up to his ankles, it was so fluffy and plush.

"You're going to *love* her!" Madison's mom told Kendall. "She'll teach you everything you need to know — which is basically everything that I taught her, of course!" She paused to wink, then went on. "I wish I could stay and see some of your skills, but I have a tennis game at one." She glanced at the gold watch on her wrist, then regretfully waved to the dog and the girls. "Bye, Herkie-Werkie, be a good boy while I'm gone. And you girls have fun! Go, Falcons!" She pumped her fist and raised a tanned knee. "Number one!"

A moment later, she was gone, though her perfume still hung in the air. Herkie was gone, too, down the hall, but his bark was still loud and clear.

"Yeah. So that was my mom," said Madison.

"She's nice. And pretty," Kendall said.

Madison half shrugged and half nodded. "She's also a little crazy." She grinned and reached for Kendall's hand. "Come on. We should go downstairs. My sister's boyfriend's coming over later, so she can only work with us for, like, an hour."

"Is Mia here?" asked Kendall.

"Oh, yeah," said Madison. "She's already down there. She spent the night."

Madison started down a hall, and Kendall followed. Cheerleaders beamed at her from both walls. They were lined up in frames, kicking and jumping, just like the Rockettes back in New York. Kendall couldn't help stopping in front of one picture of a blond girl flying and twisting in the air. Next to that was the same girl standing on top of three others, holding her leg up behind her back.

"Wow, are these all of your sister?" she asked.

Madison nodded without looking, pointing to the right. "Those are. These are my mom," she said, pointing to the left.

Kendall turned to those and noticed the difference. There were a lot more sweaters and saddle shoes. There were also a lot of vests with blue stars and tall white high-heeled boots.

"Your mom was a Dallas Cowboys Cheerleader?" She gasped.

"Uh-huh." Madison nodded as she stopped by a door. "Here," she said, opening it. "After you."

Kendall could hear the dance song from the cheer clinic blaring, as well as a strong voice counting off the steps.

"One . . . two . . . three . . . four . . . five . . . six . . . seven . . . eight! One . . . two . . . three . . . four . . . lunge . . . clasp . . . diagonal . . . punch! No, not an L! *Diagonal*, punch!"

She turned the corner, expecting to see a basement, but what she saw was something else. Not one but two walls were solid mirror, and mats completely covered the floor. The tryout video was playing on a huge flat-screen TV, and in front of it stood a blond girl, who had to be Megan, in a "Fairview H.S. Cheerleader" T-shirt and shorts.

"Hey!" She waved. "Get over here, girls! Mia needs some spirit support, I think!"

It was true. Mia did not look happy. But she did look relieved to see Madison walk in. She smiled at her, then waved to Kendall. "Hey," she panted wearily.

"This is Kendall," Madison told Megan.

"Hi, Kendall!" said Megan, flashing Kendall another toothpaste-commercial smile.

She looked so much like her mother that for a second Kendall couldn't speak. Megan didn't seem to mind, though. She shot off a baton-straight up-over-the-head kick. "What are we waiting for?" She clapped two times. "Tuck jumps! Let's go! Let's get you guys warmed up and then we'll stretch."

Before she knew it, Kendall was stretching and jumping and cheering and dancing . . . and dying to collapse onto the mat. Kendall had never worked out so hard, not even in eight years of gymnastics. As far as Megan was concerned, though, they were just getting started.

"Make sure to watch your hands. Don't make a bucket when what you want is a candlestick. And always have your thumbs outside your fists, like this. Keep your shoulders and hips square and straight. They're turning when you lunge."

"Okay," Megan said when they'd gone over the cheer and the dance a few times all the way through. "You've done it with me and with the video. Now let's see you do it on your own."

She turned off the TV, put on the music, and clapped along with the thumping beat.

Kendall took a deep breath and began . . . but by the sixth step she knew she'd messed up.

"Don't stop. Keep going!" Megan called. "If the judges see you make a strong recovery, they'll give you points for that. But, Kendall, don't count out loud, remember. Smile and do it in your head!"

Kendall was concentrating so hard she didn't even look at Madison and Mia, who were off to her right. She heard a giggle tumble out of one of them, though. Or maybe it was both.

"Seriously?" said Megan. She shook her head and crossed her arms. "Honestly, do that in tryouts, guys, and there's no way you'll make the squad."

Unfortunately, that just seemed to tickle the best friends even harder. Kendall turned to look at them at last. They were on the mats, holding hands and rolling on their backs.

"Seriously?" said Megan again.

Kendall wasn't sure what to do.

"Sorry," gasped Madison. "It's just Mia messed up and started laughing. . . ."

"I was laughing 'cause you messed up!" Mia said.

Megan sighed. "Are you done?"

Madison looked up and nodded slightly.

"Do you want me to help you guys or not?"

Madison nodded soberly this time.

"Okay. No more giggling. Or being silly. What's more serious than cheering, after all? Plus, trust me, that kind of stuff will give you a horrible score. And, Mia, stop watching Madison. You need to look — and smile — at the judges. Also, if you guys are going to try out in a group together, you're going to need to make sure your motions are all the same angle and the same height."

Were they going to try out together? Kendall hadn't realized you could choose your tryout group.

Madison and Mia had finally stopped laughing and were pulling each other to their feet. Kendall suddenly remembered Sophia and felt the tiniest bit queasy.

"Er . . . how many people can be in a tryout group?" Kendall asked Megan.

"It's up to you," Megan replied. "It could be two. It could be three. It could be four if you want."

"Oh, good." Kendall could feel the rock that had formed in her stomach start to soften up.

At the same time, a tinny cheer sounded from somewhere across the basement gym.

"Be. Aggressive! Be. Be. Aggressive! B-E! A-G-G! R-E-S-S-I-V-E!"

Megan's face changed and she ran over and swiped her phone from the top of the mini-fridge. If she hadn't been flushed already from their practice, her cheeks would definitely have been turning red.

"It's her boyfriend," said Madison. She pretended to gag.

Mia giggled and nodded knowingly while Kendall tried to form the question she wanted to ask.

"Um, if four can be in a group, then, um, could we add Sophia, do you think?"

"Sophia?" Madison glanced at Mia.

Mia bit her lip and scratched her neck.

"It's funny." Madison looked at Mia. "I never would have thought she'd be trying out."

"I know," said Mia, nodding. "It's so weird, isn't it."

"Why?" asked Kendall.

"Well . . ." Madison confirmed her answer, silently, with Mia. "She's such a *brain*."

"So?" said Kendall. "But can't you be smart and cheer?"

Madison smiled and looked at the ceiling. "That's not what I mean."

"What she means is she's quiet," Mia said.

"Right. Exactly. Thanks," said Madison. "She's quiet. And, like, super, super shy. Which, if you haven't noticed, is not exactly a great quality for a cheerleader to have. I can't really picture her on the squad, can you? Leading a cheer and hitting the crowd?"

"I don't know," said Kendall softly. "I can."

"I wonder why she's trying out," Mia said mysteriously, as if it were a crime they had to solve.

Wow. They really don't know Sophia, do they? thought Kendall.

"I think she just wanted to make some new friends," she explained with a shrug, doing her best not to sound annoyed. "And she thought it would be fun. I mean, isn't that why we're all trying out?"

"Um, no." Madison's forehead wrinkled. She was suddenly serious and stiff. "We're here to make the squad. Then we can be captains when we're in eighth grade, and hopefully varsity when we're in ninth, and then be captains again when we're seniors, and get recruited by a big, nationally ranked college who'll give us a full ride. And I'm sorry" — she crossed her arms — "but a weak middle-school tryout group is no way to start."

She finished by flicking her ponytail, which was Mia's signal to do the same.

"Now," Madison continued, "let's take a break, get a drink, and go to my room and watch TV. Do you like smoothies?" She turned to Kendall, who nodded. "Good. Mia, can you make them? With lots of pineapple and ice. I need to find Kendall a bow." She grabbed Kendall's hand. "Come on. Follow me!"

CHAPTER 6

Sophia was stretching on a mat when Kendall walked into the gym. She saw Kendall over her shoulder and smiled, but then she noticed M&M. She instantly looked surprised and curious and disappointed all at once. Kendall waved and started to walk toward her, but Madison stopped her by grabbing her arm. She and Mia headed in another direction, toward some girls Kendall had seen them talk to before. Awkwardly, Kendall glanced back at Sophia and saw another expression take hold. This one was simpler and could be summed up in one word: hurt.

Kendall felt terrible, too. So why didn't she do something? She didn't know. Instead, she let Madison pull her across the gym and smiled when she said hi to the girls Madison introduced her to.

"Everyone, have you met Kendall? She's from New York *City*," Madison said proudly. "Kendall, this is Georgia and Chandler and Sadie."

"Hi!" Georgia and Chandler and Sadie said.

They were girls who hadn't spoken to Kendall Tuesday or the day before, but now that she was Madison's friend, she wasn't invisible anymore.

There had been girls like Madison at Kendall's old school, girls who always seemed to be in charge. Kendall had been so busy with gymnastics and her own friends, though, she hadn't worried about them too much. Sometimes the girls would include her in things, and sometimes they'd leave her out. But only a few times did it bother Kendall. And only one time — that she hardly thought about — did it make her cry.

But maybe Kendall hadn't known what she was missing. Being around Madison, she thought suddenly, was a little like orbiting a star. She made you feel warm and in the spotlight. And she was hard to pull away from.

Kendall was glad when the clinic started and she could think about something else besides Sophia, across the gym. She concentrated on the warm-ups and stretches and enjoyed the compliments on her splits.

After a few minutes, she looked back and found Sophia. "Come up here," she mouthed, motioning with her hand.

Sophia shook her head. "I'm okay," she mouthed back.

"Okay, everyone!" Coach Casey eventually shouted. "Today,

instead of just going over jumps and motions, we're going to play a game! It's called Coach Casey Says! If I say 'Coach Casey says' do a motion, you do it," she explained, "but if Coach Casey doesn't say, you don't, or else you're out, just like Simon Says. Are you ready to play?" She put her hand to her ear.

"*Yes!*" answered the gym.

"Okay!" *Clap!* "Coach Casey says clean! . . . Coach Casey says touchdown! . . . Coach Casey says high V! . . . T!"

Kendall stayed in her high V, with her fists high and slightly in front, but she could see at least three girls, including Mia, snap their arms down and out to the side into a T. She watched Mia try to hide her mistake by slowly floating her arms back up.

"Ah ah ah . . . I saw that!" said Coach Casey, which wasn't very surprising, since they were standing in the front.

Mia sighed and started to sit, but Coach Casey shook her head again. "No, no, no." She grinned. "In my game, 'out' means you get up here and do the motions along with me."

It didn't take long for about a third of the clinic to move to the front with the coach. Coach Casey was good at tricking them and seemed to be having a lot of fun. She called out, "Checkmark," and pointed to Sophia, who was one of a few to hit that pose.

"Get up here," she said, smiling, and Sophia humbly obeyed.

She stood almost directly in front of Kendall, and Kendall could tell she wished she weren't. And it wasn't because of the game, either, Kendall knew. It was all because of her.

"Coach Casey says that's enough!" the coach called finally, when about ten of the sixty girls were left.

"Yeah! We did it!" Madison hopped and turned and congratulated herself and Kendall with a loud high ten.

"Okay," Coach Casey said. "Everyone back on the floor. Quickly, quickly. We're going to break into groups again, this time to go over the dance and cheer. And listen up! It doesn't have to be the same group you were in yesterday. In fact, if you have a group you want to try out with on Friday, feel free to work with them. And if you don't have a group set up yet, then start to think about it now. Look around and ask. Don't think that you're the only one who needs partners. There's always someone else. Believe me. This is a great chance to make new friends, girls. Take advantage of it! Okay! Go!"

Mia dashed directly to Madison and Kendall.

"Let's go over by the bleachers," Madison said.

Kendall looked over at Sophia, who was still standing by herself. "Uh . . . okay . . . but it looks like Sophia needs someone to practice with, too."

Madison and Mia glanced over their shoulders and exchanged *what do you want to do?* looks.

"I think she's okay," said Madison. "I'm sure someone will pair up with her." She reached for Kendall's hand, but Kendall couldn't let Sophia go.

"How about I go get her and bring her over?"

Madison looked less than thrilled. "You know," she began, waving her hand between Mia and her, "maybe it's actually better if Mia and I practice, just us two, right now."

"Oh, okay," Kendall said. This wasn't the answer she'd been hoping for.

But she felt relief, at least, when Madison slid her lip out in a pout. "We'll miss you. But we'll practice later together. Tomorrow. At my house. Come on." She hooked Mia's elbow and together they trotted off.

Kendall made her way over to Sophia and said, "Hey," with a little wave.

"Hey," Sophia said. She nodded to M&M. "When did you guys become friends?"

"Huh? Uh . . . I don't know . . ." said Kendall. "In our group yesterday, I guess."

Sophia raised an eyebrow.

Kendall swallowed. "Hey, how's your cartwheel coming?" she quickly asked. "Let me see how it looks."

Sophia shook her head. "I don't think so."

"No?"

"No. Not here. Not yet." She sighed. "I practiced. I did. And I can do a handstand now, pretty much. But the cartwheel part . . . I still come down all wrong. I don't know what my problem is."

"It'll come," Kendall assured her. "What do you want to practice right now? The cheer?"

"Sure," said Sophia.

They started by running through it slowly, step by step.

"When you make a fist, keep your thumbs out," Kendall told Sophia. "And keep your hips straight when you lunge. Don't twist."

"Thanks," Sophia said. She tried the same motions again. "Who taught you that?" she asked.

"Oh . . . huh . . . I don't know. I'm not sure." Kendall's stomach clenched into a guilty knot. She wished she hadn't lied to Sophia. She would have given anything to take it back.

"So . . . tomorrow . . ." Sophia went on. "Are you free? Want to come over again to my house?"

Tomorrow. Right. Here it was. Kendall's chance for a do-over.

And yet . . . she couldn't answer. She couldn't tell Sophia any more lies, but Madison had just asked her over, too, and it was hard to imagine turning her down. Kendall supposed she could say something came up, as she'd done with Sophia. But what if she did and Madison didn't understand? Would it mean blowing her chance to also be friends with M&M?

What was the right thing to tell Sophia? Kendall just wasn't sure. So she gave her the best answer she possibly could.

"That would be great. I want to . . ." Kendall told her, "but I'll have to ask my mom."

CHAPTER 7

"Ta-da!"

Kendall's mom placed a fresh golden-brown waffle on the counter in front of her and slid onto the neighboring stool.

"Thanks," Kendall said, feeling the steam on her chin and drawing it through her nose.

They were still eating all their meals at the kitchen island, since they hadn't picked out a table or chairs yet. The moving boxes had all been unpacked, though, and were almost completely gone, except for a few they kept around for the cats to jump into and out of.

Tiger was in one now, hiding from Lily, who was perched on the lid. He sprang up and knocked her off, and she howled and dove in after him.

Libby, meanwhile, was carefully filling each hole of her own waffle with maple syrup. "Here." She slid the sticky jug to Kendall when she was done.

"Oh . . . thanks," Kendall said again, although she didn't pick it up.

Her mom watched her sit there without moving. "Kendall, hon, something wrong? Aren't you hungry?" she asked. "Gosh, I'd think with all the cheerleading you're doing, you'd be positively starved. And even if you're not, you really need to eat." She pumped her arms as if she were waving pom-poms. "How are you going to have enough energy to ra-ra-ra?"

"We don't actually 'ra-ra-ra,'" Kendall informed her. "But I guess you're right. . . ." She took a sip of the blueberry smoothie her mom had set beside her plate. She swallowed, letting the icy sweetness coat the inside of her dry, tight throat.

"What's your plan for today, anyway?" her mom asked. "Which of your new friends are you going to see? I have to say, I'm so happy you decided to do this, Kendall. You've really met a lot of girls this week!"

Kendall looked up at her mom at last. "I don't know, Mom. That's the thing."

"What do you mean?"

"Well, Madison — that's the girl whose sister's a cheerleader — she asked me to go over there again today. But Sophia — that's the girl whose house I went to on Tuesday — she asked me to practice with her, too."

"Okay . . . So what's the problem?"

What's the problem? Kendall thought. "Don't you see?"

"No." Her mom rested her elbows on the counter. "Do you, Libby?" she asked, leaning across Kendall.

Libby licked her knife, her fork, and finally her lips. She rocked her head back and forth and licked them all again.

"Why don't you all just practice together?" her mom said. "The more, the merrier, right?"

"No, Mom, you don't understand," said Kendall. "*I'm* invited to Madison's . . . but Sophia's not. And I'm invited to *Sophia's*. But Madison and Mia aren't." Her mom had to get it now, she thought as she picked up her waffle and took a dry bite.

"Oh." Her mom nodded.

Sllluurrrrrurrrrrruurrrp. Libby sucked the last purple drops of her drink up through her straw. "Why don't you just invite them all over *here*, then?" she spoke up.

Kendall sighed and rolled her eyes. Nine-year-olds. They didn't understand girls Kendall's age any better than moms did.

"What?" said her mom. "That's a great idea. I was just about to suggest the same thing. Besides, we're finally settling in here and it'll be nice for you to take a turn hosting, since they've each had you over this week."

"I'm just not sure it would work," said Kendall.

"Why not?" asked her mom.

"Well . . . because they're *really* different," said Kendall. "I mean, they went to school together, but they're not really friends."

"Even more reason, then," her mom said.

Kendall's shoulders sagged in her frustration. She couldn't imagine what her mom meant.

"They're going to have to be friends if they make the squad," her mom said. "You'll be practicing together all the time then. Plus, think about the girls on your gymnastics team, and how different you all were. You might not have hung out with all of them at school, but just being on the team together gave you all an amazing bond."

Kendall didn't nod, but her mom was right, she knew. She thought about some of her best friends from the team. There was Lila, who was so quiet — just like Sophia — and Amber, who was not. In fact, Amber had two volumes: fire engine and jackhammer. Then there was Kylie, who'd been the best vaulter on the team but switched to ice hockey in fifth grade. She still came to all their meets, though, and even traveled with them to states.

Being on a team — even the gymnastics team, where your score was often your own — meant all for one, and one for all. A cheer squad should be just the same, Kendall realized, which was kind of why she was trying out.

"Besides," her mom said, "do *you* like them both?"

"Yes," Kendall said. She liked them both . . . though in slightly different ways. But wasn't that how it was with all friends? They all had their different strengths.

"Well, then they *do* have something in common — you," her mom declared. "So why don't you try to take it from there?"

Kendall picked up the syrup and tilted it ever so slowly over her plate. She made a puddle next to her waffle to dip it in, little by little, piece by piece.

"I guess I'll call them and see," she said. "I'll let you know what they say."

Libby, meanwhile, slid her plate toward their mom for waffle number two. "Tell them Claudia, next door, has a sprinkler," she said. "Then they'll *definitely* come!"

Sophia came over first on her bike, which was slightly too small — and a boy's.

"It was my cousin's," she explained. "I really hate it. But I'm saving up for a new one."

She and Kendall practiced cartwheels in the backyard until Kendall's mom called them in for lunch. By that time, Libby had left for Claudia's house and Kendall could hear them chasing her little brothers around next door.

"So how's the cartwheel coming?" Kendall's mom asked Kendall and Sophia as she made a sandwich for each of them.

"I'm hopeless," said Sophia.

"No, you're not!" Kendall said. "I think she's got it," she told her mom. "You just have to remember to keep your legs straight, and keep your butt up. It's not that hard."

"And when are Madison and Mia coming over?" her mom asked her.

"Any time, I think."

Sophia finished the last bite of her sandwich and made an anxious face. "So we're *really* going to practice with M&M," she said. "I don't think I've ever been alone outside of school with them. Agh. They're so good." She sighed. "I hope I don't mess up."

"Oh, don't worry," said Kendall. "They're not *perfect*." She smiled. "Well, maybe Madison is . . . but that's because her sister and her mom were both cheerleaders, too."

"Her mom was a cheerleader, too? Really?" said Sophia. "How do you know that?"

"Uh . . ." Kendall took a too-big bite of her sandwich and gulped some lemonade to wash it down. "I'm not sure," she mumbled. "It just . . . came up during practice, I guess."

Ding-dong.

"That's them," said Kendall. She slid off her stool. "Come on." She grabbed Sophia's arm.

"Thanks for lunch, Mrs. Taylor," said Sophia, hesitating. "Do you need us to clean up?"

Oops. Kendall glanced at the dishes on the counter, then at her mom.

"You're very welcome, and don't worry," her mom said. "I've got this. You all go on."

"Thanks, Mom! Come on," she told Sophia again, nodding toward the front hall. "You're going to get so good practicing with them! And we're going to have a lot of fun!"

Kendall ran to the door and opened it to see Mia and Madison, dressed in their usual matching clinic gear.

"Hi!" she said.

"Hi," they said together.

"Thanks for coming over." Kendall stepped back. "Come on in!"

Madison stepped forward, followed by Mia, and methodically she looked around.

"Nice house," she declared.

"Thanks," said Kendall. "Our old furniture looks kind of funny here, but we're getting a bunch of new stuff."

"You should call my mom," Madison said. "She's an interior decorator. She could definitely hook you up." Her eyes briefly touched on Sophia, who was standing by the stairs.

"Hey, you guys know Sophia, right?" said Kendall.

Madison nodded. Mia did, too. Sophia tugged on her ponytail and smiled.

"Hi," they all murmured after a second of what Kendall's dad would have called "dead air."

Then Madison went back to scanning the foyer, peering up the stairs and down the hall.

"So, where are we going to practice?" she asked.

"I thought we could just go outside," Kendall said.

"Outside? Really?" Madison made a disappointed face. "It's kind of hot, isn't it?"

"Well, actually," said Kendall, "it's kind of hot in here, too. You'll start to feel it in a second. Our air-conditioning's not working . . . and besides, there's not a lot of room."

"You don't have a basement?" asked Madison.

"Well, we do," said Kendall, "but it's kind of dark and gross." She decided not to go into details — such as the mousetraps and the last owner's moldy old sofa, which they still hadn't moved.

Madison sighed. "I just don't want to get sweaty. And I *really* don't want to get grass stains on my new shoes. You can get points off for exactly that kind of stuff, you know."

Really? Uh-oh, Kendall thought as she looked down at the green scuffs on her toes.

Sophia, meanwhile, bent her leg to rub a similar mark off her Keds.

Ugh. So far, so bad, thought Kendall. This practice wasn't going as she'd hoped. Madison was almost like a different person here than at her house, she thought.

And then, to make matters worse, Lily tiptoed into the foyer and wound herself around Kendall's calves. Kendall bent down to rub behind her ears, and Madison let out a yelp of distress.

"Omigosh! You have a cat!" she cried.

"Actually, I think she has two." Mia pointed to Tiger, who was slinking in, tail up, to say hello.

"What's wrong?" asked Kendall.

"I am so allergic!" Madison moaned. She suddenly sniffed and rubbed her eyes. "I knew I felt something." She opened the front door again. "Okay, fine. We're taking off our shoes and practicing outside, I guess."

Kendall hoped that once they started to practice, they'd all start to relax and have a good time. But it *was* hot. And there was no shade.

The sun hung directly overhead. Kendall began to regret the whole dumb idea even as they stretched.

They sat and each stretched her legs out to the sides in a straddle. Kendall walked her hands out in front of her and let her nose fall to the grass.

"That's it?" she heard Madison say.

Kendall twisted her head to the side to see why.

"What?" Sophia asked.

"Your legs," Madison told her. "Is that as wide as they can go? That's amazing. I didn't even know people could be so tight."

If Sophia had been a turtle, she would have yanked her head into her shell. The most she could do, however, was pull her chin into her chest.

"You'll get looser," Kendall said quickly. "Just keep stretching like you've been doing. I've seen girls tighter than you go from that to splits in weeks."

"Yeah. Too bad tryouts are *tomorrow*," Madison murmured, sucking in her lips.

From there, it just got worse. Madison made Sophia so nervous that she kept making mistakes. And the more mistakes she made, the more impatient Madison became.

"Seriously?" Madison said when Sophia skipped the second line of the cheer.

"I'm sorry," mumbled Sophia while Madison fanned herself and rolled her eyes.

Kendall spoke up. "You know what? It *is* hot. Why don't we take a break? Hey, our neighbor has a sprinkler. . . . Who wants to go over and cool off?"

She waited, but nobody answered. Instead, Madison reached for her shoes.

"What are you doing?" Kendall asked.

Madison forced a smile and picked up Mia's shoes and tossed them to her, one at a time. "Thanks for having us over, Kendall," she said, "but Mia and I have to go."

"We do?" said Mia. "What about the sprinkler? That sounded like fun."

Madison looked down and pulled at her white T-shirt. "I don't think so," she said.

"Aw." Mia shrugged. "Some other time, I guess."

"Are you sure?" said Kendall.

Madison nodded, with her back to Sophia. "Yeah. Thanks again," she said. "This has been really fun. But it's kind of hard getting a good practice in with so many *different* skill levels, you know? Plus, I *really* need to get out of the sun. My mom will kill me if I get a sunburn. Or freckles. That's even worse."

They waved, and Kendall watched their ponytails swing as they walked away.

"I guess it's just us," she told Sophia. "Sprinkler? Or more practice?" she asked.

But Sophia already had her shoes on. "Sorry, Kendall," she said, eyes down. "I think I'll go home, too."

CHAPTER 8

"I'm sorry your friends didn't stay," Kendall's mom told her in the car on the way to the clinic that afternoon. "What happened?" she asked *again*, even though every time she did, Kendall said the exact same thing.

"I don't know, Mom."

Kendall wished she could just erase the whole day and never think about it again.

"I told you it wouldn't work out," she went on.

"I just don't see why not," her mom said, "when you're all trying out for the same thing."

"You should have told them about the sprinkler," Libby chimed in knowingly from the backseat.

"I *did*." Kendall smiled over her shoulder at her sister.

"Well, then it's their problem," Libby proclaimed.

Kendall turned back around to see the middle school coming into view. Girls were ambling toward it down the sidewalk and climbing out of cars. And every single one, Kendall thought, looked like she belonged.

But do I? Kendall thought.

Kendall had felt like she did just the day before. But now she had her doubts. And not just about making the cheer squad.

Kendall thought about her old friends and what they were doing right then. Probably hanging out on Amber's roof, as Lila had texted her they might. "Amber got a baby pool and we're going to fill it up and order frozen yogurt. Wish you were here!" The roof had a furnished deck and a garden that the whole building shared, but the other tenants hardly used it, and the girls usually had it all to themselves. Life would be so much easier, thought Kendall, if she were back in New York with her friends. In fact, if her family went back now, not only could she try out Amber's baby pool, she'd be there before school started, and it would be like she'd never moved.

"Do you think Dad likes his new job?" Kendall asked her mom as they made the turn into the school.

"Yeah, I do," her mom replied, slowly stopping the car. "I mean, there's a lot of new ways of doing things to get used to . . . and it's a different audience, that's for sure."

"Do you think we did the right thing moving?" Kendall asked her. "Do you ever wish we'd stayed?"

Libby spoke up. "I don't! I love it here!" she said. "I love having a yard. And I love that there's an ice-cream man who drives right up to your house."

"We had an ice-cream man in New York that stopped on our corner," Kendall reminded her. "*And* a donut truck. Plus, I hear they deliver frozen yogurt now."

"Like Chinese food?" said Libby. "Wow. Still." She shrugged. "I like it here. Hey, look. Those girls with the bows. They're pointing at you, Ken."

Libby pointed back at Madison and Mia, who were standing about ten feet away. They had their arms linked, and when Kendall saw them, they began to wave with their free hands.

"Isn't that Madison and Maya?" Kendall's mom said as Kendall waved back at them with relief.

"It's Madison and *Mia*," she said as she pulled on the door handle. "See you later, Mom. Thanks."

"Hi." M&M greeted Kendall in unison.

"So . . . where's Sophia?" Mia asked.

Kendall chewed her lip. "She actually went home after you did. Maybe she's already inside."

"I'm sorry we left," Madison said slowly. "And I'm sorry if I made her feel bad. I just . . . I don't know . . . I just didn't think it was

82

helping anyone to keep going when she kept messing up. I'm sure she's nice and all, but as my mom says, you're either born a cheer-leader or you're not."

Kendall wasn't sure what to say to that. She looked at Mia, who seemed to feel the same way. Were they born cheerleaders? Kendall wasn't so sure. But if Madison thought so, that was good enough — she hoped.

And Madison was still talking to her, which was a huge relief. Now Kendall just had to find Sophia and make sure she was okay.

As soon as they walked into the gym, Kendall checked Sophia's usual spot. The mat was empty, though, so Kendall checked and rechecked the door as she stretched.

Soon Coach Casey stepped up in front of the bleachers and blew her whistle.

FWWWEEEEEEEEEEE!

"Good afternoon, girls!" She waved both hands. "How is every-body today?"

"Good!" the gym shouted back.

"Fabulous! Glad to hear it! Wow! I can't believe it's Thursday already, can you? We have a lot to do today — as usual! So let's get started and call the roll. Allison!"

"Here!"

And on it went . . . past Kendall . . . past M&M . . .

"Sophia!" the coach eventually called out.

She waited, then said it again.

"Sophia Arcella? No?" She made a mark on her clipboard. "Okay. Summer!" she said, moving on.

Kendall, meanwhile, put her chin on her knees and stared down at the floor. *Where is she?* Kendall wondered as Coach Casey finished calling names.

They stretched, then did some warm-ups, then Coach Casey had them gather around and take a seat.

"Before we go on, I want to go over tomorrow's tryouts," she explained, "and make sure all you first-timers know exactly how it's going to work."

First, she told them, they'd each get a number, and they'd let the judges know what groups they'd be trying out in. Then they'd wait with their groups outside the gym to be called in to perform their routine.

"When you enter, really *enter*. Don't be shy!" the coach advised. "Please, feel free to pump us up as much as you like!"

After they entered, the first thing they'd be asked to do, she went on, was to tell a little bit about themselves, then, together, they would call out the cheer.

"After that, we'll turn on the music and you'll do the dance as a group."

Finally, when the dance was complete, they'd be asked individually to do a jump.

"We could call anything — toe touch, herkie, spread eagle — so you should be ready to do them all."

She went through everything they'd be scored on: jumps, tumbling, voice, timing, motions, recovery, and poise. "And spirit!" she said, winking, hands on her hips. "Of course!"

The judges would also be scoring on appearance, she explained before going over what they should wear, which was basically what they'd been wearing all week: black shorts, white socks and white tennis shoes, and a plain — no logo — T-shirt that fit well and wasn't too big.

"The only exception," the coach said, "would be a Fairview shirt." She pointed to her own.

Madison raised her hand.

"Yes?" said the coach.

"What if you already have a uniform?" asked Madison. "Then can you wear that?"

Coach Casey shook her head, grinning. "Sorry . . . no. You'll have to wait to make the team before you can wear one of those. Oh, and no makeup!" she said, remembering, and held up a finger. "And no jewelry, please. Your hair should be in a nice, simple ponytail. And if you do wear a bow, make it white and not too big."

There was one other accessory she'd allow, she said. In fact, she hoped everyone would wear the biggest one they had.

"Who knows what I'm talking about?" she asked leaning out toward the girls.

"A smile!" they shouted back.

"Excellent! Okay." She turned to Jackie and Jordan. "How about if you two do a mock tryout for us and show everyone what it'll really be like? Would you guys like to see that?" she asked.

"Yeah!" replied the crowd.

The two cheerleaders jogged out of the gym, then ran back in with giant smiles.

"Go! Team!" they shouted. "Falcons! Win! Now!"

They stood up straight. Then Jackie did a herkie and Jordan did a hurdle — a jump that looked exactly like its name. Then — *clap!* — facing forward, they broke into the cheer.

"Who are you cheering for?

Fairview! Falcons!

Stand up and cheer once more!

Fairview! Falcons!"

Kendall found herself calling it out, too, at the same time, under her breath. It was all she could do not to jump up and motion along with them.

"Louder now! Don't be shy!

We want to hear your Falcon pride!

FAIRVIEW! FALCONS!"

At the end, Coach Casey turned on the music, and Jackie and Jordan performed the dance. They made it look so smooth and easy that when they were done, the whole gym stood up and cheered for them.

For fun, Coach Casey let the girls in the clinic call out jumps for them to do finally.

"Toe touch!"

"Double nine!"

"Pike!"

"Double hook!"

Jackie and Jordan did them all until their megawatt smiles began to fade.

"Okay, okay! Whoo. I bet those legs burn," said Coach Casey. She pretended to check her clipboard and add up a score.

"Pretty good," she said, nodding. "And if you do half as well in your tryouts" — she looked out over the clinic — "you'll make the squad for sure."

Kendall wondered if she could do even half as well. She knew a lot of the girls there could and not all would make the team. She wondered how much a back handspring or a tuck could make up for grass stains.

There was something else, though, much more important that she wondered about, too. Where was Sophia . . . and why hadn't she come?

CHAPTER 9

"Okay, everybody! That's it!" called Coach Casey. She waved her arms in wide, friendly arcs. "Go home, and tonight be sure to get a good night's sleep. You know what time to be here tomorrow, don't you?" She leaned forward and cupped her ear.

"Four o'clock!" Kendall shouted back — from her diaphragm — along with the rest of the gym.

"You got it!" The coach clapped. She then pointed with both hands at the crowd of girls. "Good job today, guys! See you then."

Madison jumped to her feet right away next to Kendall and adjusted the ends of her bow. "Practice. Tomorrow. At my house," she said as if she were announcing it on the news.

She looked at Mia, who nodded back quickly, and then at Kendall, whose nod was slower.

"I need to find out what happened to Sophia," Kendall told her. "I'm going to have to let you know."

Outside, Kendall's mom was waiting with Libby in a car full of grocery bags. She was finally starting to get used to buying a week's worth of food at one time, after years of stopping by the store every night on her way home from work, which was the way she and Kendall's dad had shopped back in New York.

"Hey, hon," she said as Kendall climbed in. "How'd the clinic go today?"

"Okay," said Kendall. She reached for the seat belt. "Except that Sophia wasn't there."

"Where was she? Was she feeling sick this morning?" her mom asked.

"I didn't think so," Kendall said. "I'm going to call her when I get home." She would have called her right then, in fact, if her phone hadn't been on the nightstand in her room at home.

"So you think you're ready for tryouts tomorrow?" asked Libby from the backseat. Her mouth sounded full, and Kendall turned to see why.

"I don't know. . . . What are you eating?" asked Kendall.

Her mom turned, too, and let out a groan. "Libby! Those rolls were for dinner tonight."

"Sorry," said Libby. "I didn't know."

"How many did you eat?" she asked.

"Two . . . and a half . . ." said Libby. She looked down at the crumbs in her hand. "Maybe three."

"I want one," Kendall said, reaching into the backseat.

"Is it okay, Mom?" Libby asked.

Their mom waved her okay. "*Now* it is. Go ahead. I'll make something else, I guess. Here, give me one, too," she said.

As soon as they got home, Kendall helped her mom carry in the groceries. Then she ran up to her room. She found her phone on top of a thick book Sophia had said she *had* to read. Kendall was already through more than half of it and totally agreed. There was a sequel, which Sophia was still reading and had promised to pass on to Kendall, too.

Kendall saw she had a text, but not from Sophia. It was from her friend Amber back in New York.

"AT THE MOVIES WITH L & K! WE MISS U!!!!!!!!!!! ☹" it said. Amber was loud even in her texts.

Kendall smiled as tears welled up in her eyes. She rubbed one away before it could fall. If she could have wished for anything right then and there, it would have been to be back with them in New York, where life was easy — unlike in Fairview. *Ha! More like Unfairview*, she thought.

And to think she'd believed trying out for cheerleading would be a good thing to do. She should have torn up the flyer, played in the sprinkler, and put off meeting people and the whole new-school thing as long as possible.

Sure, she'd had some fun. But she'd also done some things that didn't make her feel good. She didn't remember making friends being so hard, or so important, back home in New York. Plus, she had tryouts — the next day! — which she was already starting to dread.

She hadn't even told her old friends about cheerleading yet. She'd wanted to see how tryouts went. After all, what was the point of telling them only to say later that she didn't make the team?

"Miss u 2!" she wrote back right away, adding as many exclamation points as she could.

It was amazing how friends could feel so close, she thought, and at the same time so impossibly far away.

Then she called Sophia. And waited.

It took a while for Sophia to answer, but she finally did.

"Sophia! Why weren't you at the clinic?" Kendall asked in a single breath. "Oh, it's me, Kendall, by the way."

"I know," Sophia said. Her voice sounded flat. "I didn't go 'cause I'm not trying out."

"What?" Kendall heard all the words. But what they meant wasn't clear. "What are you talking about?"

She heard Sophia sigh. "I don't know what I was thinking. Madison was right. I'll never make the team," Sophia said. "So why am I even trying?"

"Don't say that!" said Kendall automatically. This was *her* fault, Kendall knew. "You've gotten so much better! And we've had so much fun. And if you don't think *you'll* make the team, then I definitely won't."

"No, that's not true at all, and you know it. You know gymnastics. I don't. It doesn't matter how much *better* I've gotten," said Sophia. "I'm still not good *enough*."

"Well, how will you know if you don't try out?" said Kendall. "Remember? The coach said it herself. It's as much about your spirit and attitude and hard work as anything else. And you've worked so hard! Forget about Madison. She doesn't know what she's talking about."

Sophia didn't say anything, so Kendall continued. "How about this," she said. "How 'bout we make a deal?"

"What kind of deal?" asked Sophia.

"We practice one more time — before tryouts tomorrow — and if you still can't do a good cartwheel, and you *really* don't want to try out, you can stay home. *But*," Kendall said, "if you're cartwheeling by four o'clock — *sharp* — then no matter what, you have to promise you'll do it with me."

She gave Sophia a half second to think about it. "What do you say? Do we have a deal?"

Kendall could almost see Sophia starting to smile as she answered. "Okay. Fine. Deal."

Kendall wasn't sure who was happier to see her the next morning — Sophia or Sophia's mom.

"I am so glad you talked her back into trying out today," Mrs. Arcella told her. "It's so not like Sophia not to see something through. And if she hadn't tried out . . . well, honestly, I don't know *what* I would have done with these. . . ." She pulled two tiny bottles out of a small drugstore bag. One was blue and one was white.

"Nail polish?" Sophia took them, looking baffled but also very pleased.

"There's a woman who lives at Brookridge that I have lunch with sometimes," her mom explained. "I was telling her about you while we ate yesterday, and how you're trying out for the squad. And that's when I found out that *her* daughter was a cheerleader, and her granddaughter, too, and that evidently all the cheerleaders are painting their nails with school colors these days . . . so, there you go. I picked some up on my way home."

"Wow, thanks," said Sophia.

"Yes, thanks so much, Mrs. Arcella." Kendall guessed she didn't know about their deal. That was fine, though, she thought, since she was sure Sophia's cartwheel would be totally cheer-worthy by four p.m.

"I thought it would be a nice thing to do for tryouts," Sophia's mom told them.

"Yeah." Sophia nodded. "I think it will."

"Good luck!" She gave them each a quick hug. "I can't wait to hear about everything when I get home!"

As soon as Sophia's mom left, the girls started stretching and practicing some jumps.

"Your straddle — I mean, *toe touch* — has gotten so good!" Kendall said.

Sophia frowned and shook her head. "But I'm hardly getting off the ground."

"I know, but your whole approach and lift and stuff are just right. You're being too hard on yourself. Remember when Coach Casey said good form was more important than height?"

When their legs started to get tired, they went back inside to get a drink.

Sophia didn't seem to want to talk about the day before, but Kendall had to say "I'm sorry," at least.

"For what? You didn't do anything," said Sophia.

"Well, it was my idea to have Madison and Mia over, and I'm sorry it was so weird. I thought it would be good to all practice together. I didn't think Madison would act like that."

"I'm sorry I made them leave," said Sophia as she poured them each a glass of iced tea.

"You didn't make them leave!" said Kendall.

"I think I did," Sophia said. "Madison's right. I'm not at her skill level."

"Neither am I," Kendall told her. "And neither is Mia, honestly."

"So you really think Madison was worried about getting freckles?" Sophia asked skeptically.

Kendall grinned and sipped her tea. "Actually, she kind of reminds me of a girl on my gymnastics team who used to get really nervous before every meet. Most of the time, she was totally cool, but when competitions came up, watch out. We learned pretty fast to just give her space and leave her alone till all the trophies were given out."

"But Madison's so good," said Sophia. "She's a hundred percent sure to make the squad."

"This girl was good, too," said Kendall. "In fact, she was probably one of our best. But she put a lot of pressure on herself . . . and she had this mom who was pretty intense. Maybe Madison's like that, too. Maybe she has a lot of pressure at home and stuff. . . ." She paused and bit her lip. "You know, I didn't tell you this, but I went over to her house to practice on Wednesday," she confessed.

"I had a feeling," Sophia told her.

Kendall set her glass down. "You did?"

Sophia dropped her chin and smiled at Kendall through a curtain of dark bangs. "I'm not exactly dumb," she said, pointing to the back of Kendall's head. "The bow?"

Kendall winced.

"It's fine. I would have gone, too, if I were you. What was it like?" Sophia asked.

"Well," Kendall said, starting slowly, "we worked pretty hard. Her sister, Megan, is like Coach Casey, actually — only a million times more tough. She taught us a lot. And they have this whole studio in their basement. It's pretty ridiculous, honestly."

"No way!"

"Way," Kendall assured her. "I think at the McElroy house it's pretty much all cheer, all the time."

"Could be worse, I guess." Sophia giggled.

"Definitely." Kendall laughed. "So. Speaking of 'all cheer' . . . shall we?" She finished her iced tea and stood up.

"Cheer or tumbling?" Sophia asked as she hopped to her own feet.

"Oh, tumbling, I think!" Kendall answered. After all, they had a deal.

They went outside and began with Kendall spotting, but she didn't need to for very long.

"You totally have it!" she told Sophia. "Your hips are exactly where they belong!"

Sophia stood, hands at her waist, grinning proudly — and panting with relief. "It feels right," she declared. Then she put her hands above her head and went for it again.

"I can't believe I couldn't do that before!" she said as this time she rounded off and clapped.

"I know!" said Kendall. "They're really not that hard." And to prove it, she cartwheeled back and forth herself.

"Show-off," Sophia teased her. "Hey, do you miss gymnastics?" she asked.

Kendall took a breath and let her head tilt. She hadn't really thought about it . . . much. "Maybe a little," she said finally. "I miss the uneven bars. Those are fun. And there's nothing in cheerleading like that, you know. But I like this whole 'squad' thing, I think. I like that all the focus isn't just on *me* — and only me — you know."

"Except in tryouts." Sophia cringed, hunching her shoulders up to her ears.

"Ugh. Don't remind me," said Kendall. "Let's keep practicing, I guess."

They went over the cheer, and after that, they practiced the dance. Kendall tried to remember for Sophia everything the coach had said about tryouts and how they would work.

"I have an idea," said Sophia. "How about if I watch you while you do a mock tryout? Then I do it, and you watch me. Then we can kind of judge each other, and make whatever suggestions we think might help."

"Great idea," said Kendall. "Have a seat and I'll go first."

Kendall wrapped up her turn with a Coach Casey *clap*. "Well?" she said, eager for Sophia's critique.

Sophia crossed her arms and chewed her lip as if she was afraid to say anything.

"Well?" Kendall said again. She wiped a little sweat off her forehead and lip.

"I don't know," said Sophia.

"What?" Kendall squeaked.

"It's just . . . those *noodle* arms of yours . . ."

"Seriously?" Kendall gasped. And she'd been concentrating so hard on keeping them tight! She frowned. Then she noticed Sophia's smile spreading.

"I'm *kidding*! That looked great," Sophia said.

"Very funny." Kendall grinned and made a play fist. "I'll show you noodle arms," she said.

Then it was Sophia's turn. Kendall watched and nodded along with the beat.

"That was good! I mean, besides your hunchback shoulders," she teased when Sophia returned to clean. "No, seriously, it was really good! My only real comment is to spirit even more and be louder. Don't be afraid to shout out the words. Your arms are as straight as dry spaghetti, but put that diaphragm to work."

Sophia nodded. "You'd think that part would be easy." She sighed. "But I get so self-conscious of my own voice."

By then it was after noon and they were exhausted — and pretty sweaty, too.

"I'm definitely going to have to go back home and change," Kendall declared, pulling at her damp T-shirt.

First, though, they sat down at the kitchen table and gave each other Fairview Falcon manicures.

"I have an idea," said Sophia. She painted Kendall's fingernails all blue. Then she added white chevrons to each one.

"I love it! It looks so professional!" said Kendall as she gently blew across the tips.

She wasn't quite as confident in her straight lines, however, so she decided to try something else on Sophia. She painted her nails all blue, too; then she painted white pom-poms on the thumbs, and when those turned out fine, she carefully spelled out F-A-L-C-O-N-S-! across the eight fingers that were left.

"If that doesn't give you spirit points, then nothing will!" she said. Sure, the *N* was a little smushed, but you could still read what it said.

At two, Kendall's mom picked her up, and she hugged Sophia good-bye.

"Thanks! And see you at tryouts, partner . . . right?" she added, just to check.

Sophia smiled. "See you at tryouts. Go, Falcons!" She waved her nails.

The letters were upside down, but really, Kendall thought, who cared!

CHAPTER 10

"I think I'm sick," murmured Kendall as the car rolled to a stop.

"Really?" Her mom felt her head. "I don't know . . . you're not hot."

"It's my stomach," Kendall said. It was doing crazy things, and no matter how hard she held it, it wouldn't settle down.

It was a feeling she'd had before, only milder, before nearly every gymnastics meet. And she guessed she'd had a version on Monday, too, before the first cheer clinic of the week. But this was *really* bad. In fact, if she hadn't promised to meet Sophia at tryouts that day, she would have been very tempted to ask her mom to turn around and drive her home.

"Are you going to throw up?" Libby asked from the back.

Kendall closed her eyes. "I don't know. I might."

"Make sure you open the door, then," said Libby, "and do it outside. One of Claudia's brothers threw up in her car one time, and you cannot get that smell out."

Her mom, meanwhile, smoothed Kendall's hair back and patted her gently on the knee. "Kendall, you're just nervous. But trust me, everyone else is nervous, too, and you're going to do great. Don't let the jitters get in the way of all the hard work you've put in this week."

"I just wish it was over already," groaned Kendall. "Why'd you let me do this, anyway?"

Her mom laughed. "Sorry. But don't forget, you've also made friends. Even if you don't make the squad — which I bet you will — you met a bunch of really nice girls."

"I know . . . but now I really want to make the squad, too."

"Well, then get in there and make it already," her mom said. She reached across Kendall and pulled on the door handle. "You sure can't make it sitting here."

Kendall sighed and heaved herself out. Her stomach did an extra flip. Her mom blew her a kiss and Kendall smiled reluctantly as she caught it and blew one back.

"My hair looks okay?" she asked, stalling.

"It looks great. Not a hair out of place."

"Good luck!" Libby called. "I know you'll make it! Mom, can I move into the front seat?"

"No. Now, Kendall, we'll be back at six with your dad, and we've already decided we're going out to celebrate, whether you make the team or not." She waved her hand as if to shoo her away. "See you then. Now go!"

Kendall joined the trickle of other girls making their way into the gym. They reminded her suddenly of grown-ups trudging into the subway in New York, all dressed vaguely alike and dreading the day at work ahead. She thought back to Monday, when they'd all looked eager and bouncy and happy and fresh. Her mom was right, she guessed. *Everyone* was nervous and tense.

Inside the gym, she could feel it, too. It was like they'd pumped in different air — or somehow sucked it out. Here and there, a few girls were stretching or practicing jumps and kicks, but most were gnawing on their nails and taking deep, shoulder-heaving breaths. It was like a gymnastics meet, but one thing was better: no leotard, at least. Shorts were *way* more comfortable — and no wedgies.

Kendall spotted Madison and Mia at almost the same time they saw her. They were two of the girls who were working on their jumps. At least, Madison was working, while Mia held on to her arms and used her own to push Madison up. Kendall waved and walked over, hoping they weren't mad that she'd practiced with Sophia instead of them.

She had thought for one millisecond — no, a nanosecond — of making up some kind of excuse. But then she realized it was their problem, not hers, if they didn't like the truth. She'd had enough of bending facts. Kendall wanted to start off a new year in a new school with as many friends as possible. But she also wanted, she realized, to be honest with everyone.

"So. Where's Sophia?" Madison stopped jumping and raised her chin to look around.

"Oh, she's coming," Kendall said, "on her bike. I went to her house, then home to take a shower. My mom just dropped me off."

"Cute nails," said Mia, pointing.

"Oh, thanks." Kendall held them up. "Sophia painted them."

"Cool!" Mia said. "We should have done that, Madison."

"We were kind of busy *practicing*," Madison reminded her. "Which we should still be doing." She glanced up at the clock. "Ugh! It's almost time. Say, Kendall . . ."

"Yeah?" Kendall watched as Madison reached back and tweaked her latest bow.

"Are you a hundred percent super sure that you don't want to try out with us? We just thought . . ." Madison paused. "Well, we just wanted to give you one last chance. I know you probably think that since you're new, you should be nice to everyone. But I would just hate it if Sophia ended up dragging down your score so that you didn't make the squad."

"Dragging down *my* score? How? What do you mean?" Kendall asked.

"I mean that your group gives an overall impression. At least, that's what my sister says."

"Which is why you'd be so great in *our* group," said Mia. "We'd be, like, a triple threat!"

"It does make sense," Madison said. "For you and for us. I mean, I don't know . . . were you thinking Sophia could make you look better or something? I guess I could see that . . ."

"No," Kendall said. "Not at all." It had never crossed her mind, the idea that she could affect someone's score, or that they could help — or hurt — hers. Sure, in gymnastics, if one girl messed up, it could lower the team's combined score. But you could always win your own gold, no matter how your teammates performed.

Madison shrugged. "Okay. Good. I'm glad. Because she won't. On the other hand, she *could* make you look worse and make you lose points."

Madison said it all so matter-of-factly that Kendall couldn't help believing it was true. And it made sense, she guessed, since the coach had made the point of how important it was for everybody's motions to look uniform.

Suddenly, a choice that had seemed simple to Kendall seemed a lot less sure. Was she really risking her chances of making the squad by being in Sophia's group?

But no. Sophia was no Madison, of course, but she'd worked hard and she knew the routines. And more importantly, they had a plan. There was no way in the world that Kendall could change it now.

"The offer stands," Madison said. "Besides, she's still not here."

Kendall suddenly realized Madison was right as she frowned and looked around. Madison's and Mia's eyes joined hers. But there was no Sophia to be found.

FFFWWWEEEEEEEE!

The whistle blew and they knew now what that meant without Coach Casey having to say a word.

All sixty — make that fifty-nine — girls moved into warm-up position and waited for her to call the roll.

Kendall glanced back toward the door again, but Sophia still hadn't arrived.

"Allison!" Coach Casey began calling as Kendall's heart started to race.

"Here!"

"Calley!"

"Here!"

"Callista!"

"Here!"

And on it went.

All Kendall could think was that Sophia had decided not to try out — *again*. . . .

She shouldn't have gone home to take a shower, Kendall thought. She should have stayed at Sophia's and done it there. Or she should have had her mom stop by Sophia's and pick her up on their way to the school.

But Sophia had seemed one hundred percent back into the tryouts. She'd practically promised to see Kendall there. What could have happened to change her mind — and leave Kendall hanging like this — in half an afternoon?

"Kendall!"

"Uh . . . here!" Kendall tried to shout, but it came out hoarse and thin.

The coach made a funny, mildly startled face.

She went on, though, and came to "Sophia."

She waited, but there was no "here."

Kendall could see Madison and Mia trading raised eyebrows. They seemed to be trying not to grin.

"Sophia?" Coach Casey called out again, meanwhile. This time she frowned, looking out at the gym.

"Here!"

Sophia?

Kendall whipped around to see her standing, looking winded and red, in the very back row. Sophia inhaled and held her breath, waiting for Coach Casey to move on.

Kendall was so relieved that she forgot to be nervous for the rest of roll call. Then, of course, it was time for the actual tryouts, and Kendall's stomach quickly turned back into a Tilt-a-Whirl.

"This is it!" *Clap!* "The big day! Everybody ready?" Coach Casey punched out a V.

"Yeah!"

"We're ready!"

"Let's go!"

The whole gym erupted in eager, nervous energy.

"All right! Yes! Me too! You made it through the week, and now it's time for all your hard work to pay off! And listen, girls, no matter *who* makes the squad this year, seriously, you should all be proud of yourselves for the awesome commitment each and every one of you has already shown. Honestly, I wish I could have a team big enough to take all of you," she said. "But, well, it gets kind of awkward if the cheer squad is larger than the football team, I'm afraid."

She crossed her arms and gazed around the gym slowly. "Now we're going to give you all numbers and send you out into the hall. It's fine if you want to practice out there, or just sit and relax and psych yourself up. But be sure, whatever you do, to conduct yourselves like the model citizens — and sportswomen — all cheerleaders are. Now, here comes the nitty-gritty. Pay close attention, everyone."

She explained how they would be asked to come in group by group to execute the cheer and dance. "Then we'll ask you, individually, to show us some jumps, and, if you can do them, any tumbling stunts. These are in no way expected, mind you, but they can earn you extra points. Then, when all the groups have performed, my fellow judges, Jackie and Jordan, and I will tabulate all the scores, and very simply, the top seven eighth graders, top seven seventh graders, and top six sixth graders will be invited onto this year's squad. In addition, the next-highest scorer from each grade will be named an alternate, *which* means just as much commitment to the squad, just so we're clear. Alternates *will* make every practice, and every game, as well. If someone gets sick or injured — or cut — we'll need you to be ready immediately to fill in."

As the coach spoke, Kendall let her eyes travel up and down the rows of girls. At least, she thought, she wasn't competing against the seventh or eighth graders, especially the ones like Ella and Natasha, who'd been on the squad before. But how many of the girls there were sixth graders? she wondered. She wasn't sure, but she had a feeling a lot were. And just six spots wasn't very many — especially if two were already taken, as they were sure to be, by M&M. That left four. So what were the chances that she and Sophia could get half of those?

While Kendall chewed the inside of her cheek and wrung her hands behind her back, Coach Casey waved Jackie and Jordan toward her, then looked around and clapped.

"You guys look nervous." She grinned. "I know just how you feel. How 'bout let's all take a deep breath?" She inhaled slowly, raising her arms above her head. Kendall and the other girls followed, and exhaled with her, lowering their arms to their sides again.

"And now I don't know a better way to get us all pumped up and ready to show our spirit than to go through the cheer one more time, all together. Jackie? Jordan? What do you think?"

"Let's do it, Coach!" They beamed and bounced to attention, fists on hips, ready to go.

"How about you guys?" Coach Casey pointed to the rows before her.

"Let's do it!" the gym yelled back, snapping to clean position.

"Well, then let's hit it!" Coach Casey shouted. *Clap!*

"Who are you cheering for?

Fairview! Falcons!

Stand up and cheer once more!

Fairview! Falcons!

Louder now! Don't be shy!

We want to hear your Falcon pride!

FAIRVIEW! FALCONS!"

"Amazing!" said Coach Casey when it was over. And she was right. They sounded great.

And it worked, Kendall realized. She really *was* pumped up!

"Okay! Head over to the doors and get your numbers!" called Coach Casey.

Madison turned to Kendall. She suddenly looked a little pale. "Last chance," she said. But she didn't seem surprised when Kendall shook her head. Madison took a deep breath and linked elbows with Mia. Ponytails swinging, they marched away.

"Sophia!" Kendall waved and ran over to her. "What happened? Where *were* you?" she asked.

Sophia tossed her head back and groaned. "You won't believe it," she said. "I got a flat tire on the way! I knew I didn't have time to go back and get my scooter, so I literally had to run with my bike for a mile." She wiped the lingering sweat off her neck and forehead, up into her hair. "So much for the shower I took, huh? Ugh." She looked down. "Do I look like a total mess?"

"No, you're fine. You can clean up in the bathroom," said Kendall. "I have a brush you can use in my bag. I'm just glad you're *here*. I was so worried. I thought maybe you'd changed your mind again."

Sophia lowered her chin and looked up through her lashes and her clumped, damp bangs. "I may chicken out *once*," she told Kendall, half smiling. "But never, ever twice."

By then, they'd reached the door, where Jackie was giving out numbers and safety pins.

"Kendall . . . you're number thirty-three. And, Sophia . . . let's see . . . you're fifty. Cool. Here, you need to put these on the front of your shirts. So," she asked after they'd gotten their numbers, "who'll be in your group?"

"Uh, just us," Kendall and Sophia said.

"Great!" Jackie wrote that down. "Okay." She quickly scanned the list. "The coach likes to start with sixth graders. How would you guys like to go first?"

Kendall was almost afraid to look at Sophia, but Sophia had already turned to her. Could they say *No, thank you, how about last instead*? Kendall wondered. She had a feeling they didn't have a choice.

Sophia slowly turned back to Jackie. "Do I have time to fix my hair?"

Jackie nodded encouragingly and waved them out to the hallway. "Oh, yeah. For *sure*. I was going to tell you to do that."

CHAPTER 11

They had ten minutes, Jackie told them. Ten minutes before Kendall and Sophia had to go back into the gym. Ten minutes before they'd see, finally, if they were truly squad material.

They dashed to the girls' room, just outside the gym doors, gripping their bags and each other's hands. There were already a bunch of girls inside, including Ella, Natasha, and Kiki, who were clustered together in front of one mirror, expertly primping each other's bows. Ella's boot was off, and her cheer shoes looked brand new and sparkling white.

"Hey," Ella said as Kendall and Sophia burst in. "Slow down. What's the big rush?"

"We're first," said Kendall.

"Oh." Ella's mouth formed a ring around her gap.

"How'd *that* happen?" asked Kiki.

"I don't know." Kendall shrugged.

"Is that bad?" Sophia gulped.

Ella sucked her O in and shrugged, but Natasha shook her head quickly.

"I say it's good," said Natasha. "You can get it over with. You don't have to sit around and wait for your turn."

"That's true," Kiki agreed. She sighed. "I feel like the longer we wait, the better the chance that I'll get sick."

"Okay. Stop," said Ella. She took Kiki's shoulders and leaned toward her until their noses nearly touched. "You need to take three deep breaths . . . Are you listening?"

Kiki's nose brushed hers, up and down.

"Do this," said Ella. "Take a deep breath and say, 'I know I can do this.'"

Kiki obeyed. "I know I can do this." She breathed.

"Good. Now do that three more times — with spirit!" Ella said.

"I am going to do this! I'm going to do this! I'M GOING TO DO THIS!" Kiki yelled.

Kendall, meanwhile, fished through her bag and pulled out a brush for Sophia to use.

"Here." Natasha waggled her finger at Sophia. "Come here and let me help you out. Wow, you have pretty hair," she said as she expertly swept it all up into a high, tight ponytail.

Kendall fiddled with her own bangs, but there wasn't much more she could do to her hair. She checked her socks, then yanked out her T-shirt and carefully tucked it back in.

Ella watched her and pulled her mouth sideways.

"What's wrong?" Kendall asked.

Ella reached out and loosened Kendall's shirt a little. "Better," she declared. "That looked kind of weird."

"Thanks," Kendall said. "Should we go?" she asked, since Natasha was done with Sophia's hair.

Sophia took a deep breath and nodded.

"Good luck!" said Natasha, slipping the brush into Kendall's bag.

"Thanks," Sophia and Kendall said together.

"Hey, remember to show spirit from the minute you enter," said Ella. "And be sure to smile the whole time. I know some girls don't start till they start calling the cheer, and you can totally lose points for that."

"It's true. I think that's been one of my problems," said Kiki. "The first year, I started out smiling, but then I messed up and got all upset and started to cry. Then last year" — she shook her head — "I was so happy when I *didn't* mess up —"

"She started to cry about *that*!" Ella cut in with a laugh.

"They were tears of joy," Kiki explained, blushing.

"Yeah, the judges didn't quite get that, I guess." Ella squeezed Kiki's shoulder and sighed. "You'll get it right this time and rock it, I know," she said. "And let us know how it goes," she told Kendall. "I'm sure you guys will do awesome. I know you'll make the squad!"

Kendall waved and reached for the door, but it suddenly swung open, almost into her face. Mia pushed in from the other side, leading Madison by the arm.

"Is she okay?" Kendall asked as Madison lunged for the nearest stall.

"I think so," said Mia. "She was fine — great — just a second ago. I think . . . I hope . . . it's just nerves."

"Gosh . . . I hope she feels better," said Kendall, as the battleship-gray stall door banged closed.

"Me too," mumbled Mia, who was beginning to look queasy herself.

"We're up first," Kendall explained, sliding past her, out the door. "Good luck," she told Mia. "Feel better, Madison," she called.

The door closed behind them.

"Wow, she looked *nervous*," said Sophia.

"I know — hey, are *you* okay?" Kendall looked at Sophia, who was pulling on her hair so hard it looked like her ponytail might break away.

"I'm thinking about that cartwheel. . . . I'm not going to do it. I'm too afraid that I'll mess up."

"What? No!" Kendall stopped in the middle of the hall. "You have to do it!" she said.

"No. I don't." Sophia shook her head. "And I'm not."

"Yes, you are!" Kendall said, trying to sound confident and firm. At the same time, though, Madison's warning crept into the back of her mind: *She could make you look worse and make you lose points. . . .* Could a missed cartwheel do that? Would it be better for both of them, Kendall wondered, if Sophia *didn't* try one after all?

"Are you guys ready?" Jackie called to them from the doors to the gym.

Kendall and Sophia froze. They grabbed each other's hands.

"Ready," they said together.

"Here comes group one, Coach!" yelled Jackie, pushing the doors open with her back.

As they followed, Kendall pulled Sophia close. "I still think you should do the cartwheel," she whispered. "But it's up to you. Just, no matter what, don't forget to be loud, and smile."

Sophia squeezed her hand. "You too."

They jogged into the gym and up to the table where Coach Casey and Jordan were already sitting. Jackie slipped into the chair on the coach's other side. The judges smiled expectantly, as if they couldn't wait for what came next.

"Go! Team!" Kendall shouted. She kicked and did a tuck jump.

"Go, Falcons!" Sophia chanted in a voice not quite as loud.

She pumped her arms and kicked. "Win!" she yelled, much louder this time.

"Yes! I like it!" The coach nodded warmly, and Kendall could suddenly see her in the library, approving of some great book she had picked out. "Let's see. . . ." Coach Casey glanced down at a sheet of paper on the table and laced her fingers up under her chin. "Okay. Number thirty-three, tell me a little bit about yourself, please."

"Um . . . okay!" Kendall stepped forward, took a deep breath, and stood up super straight. "My name's Kendall . . . Kendall Taylor," she added, "and I'm in sixth grade. And I actually just moved here this summer from New York, New York. It's so nice they named it twice, you know!" She gulped. Where had *that* come from? "I like music, and gymnastics, and movies, and chocolate — except the kind with cherries — and just about every animal in the world. And I love trying new things — like cheering — which has been really, really fun!"

Was that enough? She tried to think of something else to add, but Coach Casey spoke up, happily, before she could.

"I couldn't agree more! And welcome to Fairview, Kendall. I love that you just moved here and jumped right into these tryouts. Good for you! I hope you've met a lot of new friends."

"Oh, it's been great!" Kendall peeked over her shoulder at Sophia. "I totally have."

"Awesome! Now. Number fifty." Coach Casey's eyes shifted to Sophia. "Let's hear about you, if you please!"

Kendall felt Sophia step up beside her. "Hi . . . I'm Sophia Arcella," she said. "I'll be in sixth grade, too."

"Sophia *Arcella*?" Coach Casey leaned forward on her elbows. "Is your mom, by any chance, the nurse?"

"She is," said Sophia.

"Mrs. Arcella! I *love* her!" Jordan exclaimed.

"Oh, yeah!" Jackie said. "Me too!"

"Tell her hi," Coach Casey told Sophia. "And go on. Sorry to interrupt!"

"Oh, that's okay," said Sophia. "Well," she continued, "I like reading and puzzles and taking pictures and I was the junior state chess champion two years in a row. But . . . well, those are all great, but they're so . . . solitary. I'm here because . . . because I really want to be part of a group."

This made Jackie and Jordan smile at each other, while Coach Casey lowered her hands. She picked up a pencil, then made sure that Jackie and Jordan had theirs ready, as well.

"Shall we begin?" she said. "Cheer first — as you know. We're ready when you are. Okay? Fire us up!"

Kendall took a deep breath and looked at Sophia, who quickly nodded.

"Ready. Hit it." And together they clapped.

"Who are you cheering for?"

Louder! Kendall reminded herself . . . and Sophia, too.

"Fairview! Falcons!"

Better! she thought. *From the diaphragm . . . Lunge — toe up!*

"Stand up and cheer once more!"

Wrists tight . . . Check . . .

"Fairview! Falcons!"

Keep hips straight and punch*! Elbow to ear . . .*

"Louder now! Don't be shy!"

Left L . . . no right L! Phew! That was close. . . .

"We want to hear your Falcon pride!

"FAIRVIEW! FALCONS!"

And it was done!

Kendall and Sophia ended, together, back in clean position, still all smiles.

Right away, Sophia fired off a kick — almost to Kendall's surprise. "Let's go, Falcons!" she shouted.

Way to go, Sophia! Kendall thought.

Feeding off her spirit, Kendall bounced on her toes. "Yay! Falcons!" she yelled. "C'mon! Go!"

She punched out a high V and let her fingers spirit out and down.

"Hey, good spiriting." Coach Casey grinned and made some notes on her sheet. Jackie and Jordan nodded and leaned over the table to do the same.

Kendall's eyes met Sophia's and winked.

Coach Casey leaned back in her chair. "Okay. Now on to the dance. Jordan, is the music ready? Great! Ready, girls?"

She sat there looking at them, waiting, Kendall realized, for a reply.

"Yes, Coach!" she shouted.

"Oh, yes, Coach!" Sophia yelled.

Coach Casey gave them an appreciative thumbs-up. Then she signaled Jordan to start the song. The music began . . . and so did the girls.

And it was great!

That is, until the second eight count, when Kendall started to repeat the first. She caught herself almost immediately — but she could feel her cheeks starting to burn. *Don't stop, don't make a big deal*, she told herself — over and over. *Just keep going and don't make it worse!*

She put it behind her and worked even harder to make the rest of the dance as perfect as it could be. They ended, knees up, and as the music stopped, they slowly brought them down.

Almost there, Kendall thought. Some jumps and tumbling and they'd be done!

"Really good! Okay. Number thirty-three." The coach tapped her pencil on the table. Her fingers slid down the yellow sides. "Would you please do a toe touch for us?"

"Sure . . . Yes!" Kendall said.

She stepped forward and lifted her arms, then rose up on her toes. She swung her arms down on the next count and wound up into the jump.

Phew! Kendall thought as she landed, knees bent, hands by her sides, and popped back into clean. It wasn't that high a jump, but it was tight, at least. She hoped the coach noticed how much she'd worked on that since the beginning of the week. If Coach Casey had, however, she didn't say anything.

What she did say was "Thank you! Now, any tumbling? If you'd like to show us something, this is the time. You told us you like gymnastics. . . . Any skills you'd like to demonstrate for us?"

"Definitely!" said Kendall. She straightened her back and pointed her toe. She took a breath and rounded off into a back handspring, followed by a tuck.

Jordan started clapping. "Jackie," she said, leaning sideways, "that was as good as yours!"

"It sure was. *Nice!*" said Coach Casey. "Okay. Number fifty, it's your turn. Will you do a spread eagle, please?"

"Okay." Sophia stepped forward, wound up, and jumped.

Kendall thought it was the best that Sophia had ever done.

"Thanks. Excellent," said Coach Casey. "Now. If there's any tumbling *you'd* like to show us, here's your chance. Feel free."

Kendall looked at Sophia and could see she was struggling with the choice she had to make. She was smiling, but it was stiff and didn't quite make it to her eyes. Kendall nodded encouragingly. It was all she could do not to yell, "Do your cartwheel! Please!"

"I . . . I can do a cartwheel," Sophia said.

Yay! Kendall automatically clapped.

Sophia turned to her, smiled, took a deep breath, and raised her hands.

Oh, no . . . Kendall thought the second her hands came down together. What had she done? Mistake number one! There was no way to pull off her cartwheel after that, Kendall knew, and she winced as Sophia's legs fell clumsily down, one by one. Kendall had to give her a *lot* of credit after that for not losing her smile as she stood up.

"Okay. Thank you so much, Sophia. Kendall. Jackie, let's call in the next girls."

"Wait!" Kendall's hand shot into the air before she could keep it down. "Please! Coach! Can she do it again? She can do a great cartwheel — I've seen her. Could you let her try?"

Jackie and Jordan looked fairly shocked. But Kendall didn't care.

Her eyes were on Coach Casey, who looked startled but as if she also liked the idea.

The coach laid her pencil down, and Kendall imagined her saying yes.

"I'm sorry — I know I didn't say this before, but we don't do retries," she said instead. "Of course, I understand we don't all hit everything perfectly every time, but we have so many routines to review, we just can't. Thanks again, girls." With that, she smiled and waved while Jackie hopped up and jogged across the gym.

CHAPTER 12

"I'm so sorry," said Kendall.

"What for?" asked Sophia. "You didn't mess up my cartwheel. I knew I would. And I did."

They were sitting in the hall, toe to toe, knees up under their chins. All around them, clusters of girls waited for their turns to go into the gym. Some were quiet and some were noisy, some looked dazed, and some couldn't keep still.

"How'd it go?" one group had asked Kendall as they walked out.

"Okay," she'd said. Then she saw Sophia's face. "Sophia? What's wrong? It wasn't that bad."

Now she felt terrible for urging Sophia to do that cartwheel. She wished more than anything she could take it back.

"Remember," she told her. "It was just optional. It can't hurt you. It was just for extra points. And you didn't even need them because everything else you did was so good."

"But it wasn't," said Sophia. "Didn't you see me mess up the dance? That's why I decided to do the cartwheel — to make up for that."

"Oh . . . no . . . I didn't see anything!" said Kendall. "I guess I was too busy messing up myself. I just wish they would have let you try it again. I know you could have done it if you went back and fixed the start."

Sophia tapped Kendall's toes with her own. "Thanks for asking them . . . and thanks for trying out with me. It's so not your fault. And no matter what, it was a pretty fun week."

There wasn't much more to say until the rest of the groups had gone. Madison and Mia came out of the bathroom before too long, looking better, but still not great.

"Are you okay?" Kendall asked, looking up at Madison as she walked by.

She nodded. "Of course I'm okay." Then she lifted her chin and tightened her bow and smiled off into space.

"Are *you* okay?" Kendall asked Mia, who was following her, nibbling busily on a fingernail.

She shrugged. "I'm okay if she's okay. . . . Madison, don't worry, you're going to crush it," she called to her.

They were next, and Jackie led them in. About five minutes later, they came out.

"So? How did I do?" Kendall heard Madison ask Mia.

"Awesome!" Mia assured her. "You were great."

"Okay. Good." Madison shut her eyes and leaned back against a bulletin board.

"How'd I do?" Mia asked her.

"Good, I think," said Madison. "But you were standing behind me the whole time, so I couldn't really see." She opened her eyes and looked at Kendall and Sophia. "Your tryout went okay?"

"It went pretty well," Kendall said.

"Except for my cartwheel," Sophia chimed in.

"Except for her cartwheel," said Kendall. "I asked them if she could try it over, because she really can do one, you know. But I guess that's not how it works." She sighed. "Oh, well. Now we know."

Madison bent forward, splitting from the wall. "You asked them *what*?" she said.

"If she could do it again . . . ?"

"Eek." Madison curled her lip. "I hope they don't take off points for that."

"For what?" asked Kendall.

"For talking back."

"Would they do that?" Kendall reached down to hold on to the floor. It suddenly felt like it would crumble and fall away.

Madison shrugged. "I don't know. You'll find out, I guess." She grabbed Mia's hand. "C'mon. I just remembered, I have to text my mom," she said.

Kendall turned back to Sophia, who at first looked worried, but shook it off.

"They wouldn't take points off for that," she told Kendall. "The coach was really nice. Besides, your tumbling would more than make up for any points they took off if they did."

Kendall put her forehead to her knees. "Ugh. This is torture, don't you think? At least in gymnastics, they gave you your score right away and you knew exactly where you stood. Who knew this part of tryouts would be the hardest of all?"

But at last, it was over — almost — and Natasha, Ella, and Kiki burst out of the gym. They were the last group, and from their hugs and high fives, the others could see that their tryout had gone well.

"Guys, we'll have scores in pretty quickly," Jackie said. "Just sit tight and wait. Congratulate yourselves, go get something to drink, whatever, and the coach will be out in a few minutes with *the list*." She flashed two thumbs up, then ducked back into the gym.

As promised, a few minutes later, Coach Casey stepped through the door.

"Okay." She smiled as all the girls in the hall scurried toward her like ducklings desperate to be fed. She waited a second for the last ones, hugging her clipboard to her chest. "Thank you for your patience. And for all your hard work this week," she said. "What I'm going to do now is call out the numbers of the athletes who made the squad. If you hear yours, please go into the gym. I'll wait to call the three alternates at the end. If I don't call your number, when I'm done, then" — she cocked her head — "you're free to go. But you should be proud of yourselves for just coming to these clinics and for the devotion you've shown all week. And I want you to know that we didn't see anyone here who couldn't come back with some more prac- tice and very well make the squad next year." Jackie and Jordan, who were standing behind her, nodded emphatically. "Unless, of course, you're an eighth grader, in which case" — the coach held up an *aha* finger — "there's the high-school team!"

Coach Casey inhaled. "Okay." She held up her clipboard. "Thirty . . ."

Kendall tensed.

". . . six."

Kiki jumped up and about half the hall broke into a cheer.

"Okay, okay, moving on . . . Two."

Girl by girl, the crowd thinned out as the new squad broke away. Kendall noticed it getting quieter, too — so quiet she could hear the girls around her wringing their hands and sucking their teeth.

"Fifty."

Sophia?

Yes!

Kendall turned and hugged her. Sophia seemed too stunned to move.

"Get up! Get in there!" Kendall said, giving her a needed push.

"Oh, right!" Sophia stumbled to her feet. "I'll see you soon!" she said, pointing to Kendall as she followed number seven — Ella — into the gym.

There were still plenty of numbers to go, but the faces of the girls left were getting tense. The most anxious of all, by far, was Madison's, though Kendall knew she'd make the team. Mia, meanwhile, sat beside her, patting her shoulder now and then.

"Forty."

"Finally!" Madison jumped up.

Mia sprang up, too, and hugged her tight.

Madison's whole face, her whole *body*, changed instantly, as if some spirit had been exorcised.

"Yes!" She clapped and let Mia hug and congratulate her again.

"You're next!" Madison told her as she skipped into the gym.

But Mia wasn't. And neither was Kendall.

Instead, four other girls were called, which left — Kendall knew, since she'd been counting — exactly one more to fill the squad.

She locked eyes with Mia, who seemed to realize the same thing. Instead of looking worried, though, she crossed her arms and looked annoyed.

Oh, well, Kendall told herself. So she didn't make it. A lot of girls didn't. That was okay. Like the coach said, if she really wanted to, next year, she could try out again.

Oh, be quiet, she told that voice inside her. She wanted to be a cheerleader *this* year. Really bad! She had to bite her lip hard not to cry.

"Thirty-three."

Nobody stood up.

Thirty-three! That was *her* number, Kendall realized.

She had made it?

Yes, she had made it!

She had made the squad!

She got up and was instantly glad not only that she'd made it, but that she'd been sitting so close to the door. She could feel all forty other girls staring at her, and she knew without even looking that they were all wishing they were her.

"Welcome to the squad." Coach Casey patted her shoulder as Kendall passed her to join the others in the gym.

"Kendall!"

The second she walked through the door, Sophia hugged her, and the girls standing behind her cheered. Everyone, that is, but Madison, who looked as if someone had just told a joke she somehow didn't get.

She was silently counting the girls with her finger. Then a lost look came over her face as the truth sank in that the squad had been filled, and Mia wasn't in there with them.

Sophia seemed to notice it, too. Her eyes met Kendall's, wide with shock. They were *M&M*. How could they not both be on the squad?

Then, suddenly, the door opened and three more girls — the alternates — came in with the coach.

The last one was Mia.

Madison held up her hands as if to say *What happened?*

Mia shrugged and did the same.

Coach Casey, meanwhile, waved the brand-new team toward her.

"Congratulations!" she said as they gathered around. "Welcome, new athletes, to the squad! And to all you veterans, I missed you! It's so good to have you back! We have a lot to go over now, natu-rally, but a lot of it can wait until next week, when I will see you all back here for the start of training camp — same time, same place. We have a *lot* to practice and learn before the first football game in two weeks!"

She went on, and though Kendall listened, her mind began to race. This wasn't just the start of something new for her, she realized. There was a very good chance that from this moment on, her whole life was going to change!

Stand up and cheer for more Squad!

Sophia's made the squad — but will she be leaving her old friends behind?

Confectionately Yours

Don't miss all the books in this delicious series!

For anyone who's ever felt that boys were a different species . . .

Twelve-year-old Kara McAllister has a great idea: The Boy Project! By making charts, graphs, and taking notes on different boys, she's sure to find the right guy for her.

If only it were that easy . . .

"A rollicking ride through middle-school affairs of the heart." —*Booklist*

"Kinard creates a highly credible middle-school universe of popular girls, dorky boys, unpredictable teachers, and volatile loyalties; she hits all the right notes . . ." —*Publishers Weekly*

POISON APPLE BOOKS

The Dead End

This Totally Bites!

Miss Fortune

Now You See Me...

Midnight Howl

Her Evil Twin

Curiosity Killed the Cat

At First Bite

THRILLING.

BONE-CHILLING.

THESE BOOKS

HAVE BITE!